ONE PRINCE
TWO
KINGDOMS

JANA GRISSOM

ONE PRINCE
✦—— TWO ——✦
KINGDOMS

TATE PUBLISHING
AND ENTERPRISES, LLC

Published by Tate Publishing & Enterprises, LLC
127 E. Trade Center Terrace | Mustang, Oklahoma 73064 USA
1.888.361.9473 | www.tatepublishing.com

Tate Publishing is committed to excellence in the publishing industry. The company reflects the philosophy established by the founders, based on Psalm 68:11,
"The Lord gave the word and great was the company of those who published it."

Book design copyright © 2015 by Tate Publishing, LLC. All rights reserved.
Cover design by Jan Sunday Quilaquil
Interior design by Jimmy Sevilleno

Published in the United States of America

ISBN: 978-1-62854-197-7
Fiction / Fantasy / General
15.02.16

DEDICATION

To my forever love, Roy, who has
always believed in me.

To my awe-inspiring children, Kaylee and
Cody, who I love more than anything.

To my foster children, who I will
remember and love forever.

To my parents, Devon and Diane, who have
edited and encouraged my writing to completion.

ACKNOWLEDGMENTS

THE WORDS IN this book were designed to comfort my foster children who were afraid. I created an imaginary world where their extraordinary foster family could and would protect them from any dangers. Each night, before we went to sleep, we would read a new chapter that I had written, hoping to help reduce the nightmares. Eventually, the nightmares were replaced with laughter and anticipation of the adventures of a foster kid, Johnny Boggs, who was just like them.

Each chapter was inspired by my children, Kaylee and Cody. Memories of their escapades at school and at home translated on to paper to create the journey Johnny would face. When I would have times of writer's block, my kids would sit down for an interrogation from Mom and provide ideas from their experiences for my writing. Thank you, Kaylee and Cody, for making this book fun and authentic because you were willing to support me throughout its creation.

To all my PASS students from Godley Middle School, thank you for the inspiration and memories. It was a pleasure teaching and getting to know each one of you as unique individuals. This book has many outstanding characters because of you. Go, Wildcats! Thank you McKenzee, Oren, Ben, and Noet for reading and critiquing 1P2K! Teresa Beck, you are an amazing teacher and friend. Thank you for being my final critique and comma hero. I wouldn't have finished it without your help and encouragement!

Over the years, I changed and edited this book numerous times. Frustration would set in, and I would put the book away. My wonderful husband believed in me and continued to prompt the completion of my first novel. Thank you, Roy, for being the best husband who truly loves me!

To my first editors, Mom and Dad, thank you for reading, rereading, and rereading this book to provide valuable input and corrections. You both have inspired and encouraged me throughout my entire life that I can do anything I put my mind to. If it were not for you, Mom and Dad, then I would probably still be working on this book today.

Finally, thank you to Tate Publishing and the entire staff who have made this book happen. Words cannot express my gratitude to you all for believing in my manuscript and making it come to life.

CONTENTS

GONE

I'M SLEEPING, BUT I'm awake, standing in the main hallway of our house staring at the front door as if someone just left, or maybe they're about to walk in.

My eyes tilt toward a faint blue light revealing a curvy silhouette leaning against the wall. I smile and straighten my T-shirt. Before I work up the nerve to actually say something, blue fingers of light twist their way out from under the hall closet door and wrap around her body before finally illuminating her vaporous eyes.

My breath chokes me.

I jerk my eyes to the floor along with my stupid grin. There's no way! I lift my head right back up, needing to see her eyes one more time, but I stop at her mouth.

Her lips are frozen in a seductive smile as her voice calls to me, "Johnathon."

She glides in a boneless motion toward me. The blue light responds to her movement, billowing around her like a silk robe hanging off her shoulders and sliding down her back.

Blood rushes to my muscles, preparing to get the heck out of here, but something about her makes me want to stay. I just stand there and stare.

Without warning, the light within her strikes at my face like a snake, sinking its teeth into my neck and wrapping its muscular body around my head.

I should've run.

My nostrils flare, sucking in oxygen as my brain flashes images of her eyes. I struggle to peel its body off my mouth and neck as it drags me across the floor to the hall closet. Without a touch on the handle, the door flies open. My heart beats hard against my chest. I kick and twist against nothing, hoping to find its weakness, but the more I struggle, the tighter the light constricts.

Fighting is useless.

I stop moving as if the battery inside suddenly lost all power. At that very moment, the light opens its mouth and swallows me whole, dropping me at least twenty feet through its portal onto the rock-hard ground below. The impact knocks every bit of oxygen out of my lungs. I gasp and suck in a plume of hot, thick air as if the building around me is on fire. I grab my chest and pull at my shirt. My eyes dart around, desperate to find a way out of here.

"You cannot hide him forever!" screams a woman.

My muscles jerk. I turn and see a beautiful woman wearing a black leather dress with black vines wrapping up her neck and twisting into a crown covered in black diamonds, Queen Nara.

This is not good.

I scan the room for a way out, hoping to locate a hallway or even a small crack in the stone to force myself through. Motion catches my eye in the shadows behind the queen. There's an army of Troglodytes, the beasts of darkness, shifting and grunting as they descend the stone wall, hungry for orders. To the queen's right stands three guys and three girls each wearing a crown of black diamonds, but to her left stands a huge man, the only one without a crown. He's staring me down with black, empty eyes, a hollow man wringing his hands, ready to tear me apart as if he already despises me. I try to army crawl backward, but my feet hit a wall.

There's no way out.

A few feet from me, another woman growls, "You will never take *my* son!"

I'd know that growl anywhere. A thin smile spreads across my face; it's my mom. If she's here, then I'm sure the Guardians are too. I turn to see how many stand beside her, but she's alone. In fact, my mom's moving into her fight stance as if she's going to fight a million Trogs and the frickin' Queen of Darkness all by herself. What is she thinking? My chest tightens. Mom steps back and glares into the beautiful queen's inhuman eyes.

Queen Nara confines her laugh to a chuckle. "You don't understand. He's already mine." She twists her neck around. The vines follow her movement, crawling down her leg and cracking through the soil as they move across the room and reveal what's hiding on the ground behind my mom—*me*.

I sit up, hoping for the sudden power of invisibility, but the only power I have is holding back the puke trying to force its way up.

Mom's muscles jump under her skin. With no time to think, she surrounds herself in a bright light and leaps toward Queen Nara. The queen lifts her hands, casting a fog that surrounds Mom's orb and clenches her light so tightly it bursts. Mom collapses to the ground right in front of me, covered in tiny cuts from the shattered orb as if it were made of glass.

I lunge forward to help her, but Mom reaches out and stops me. "Johnny, you have to get out of here before it's too late."

She clutches her chest as it heaves up and down gasping for air. I grab her arms and use all of my strength to try to pull her up, but she motions for me to wait. Mom drops back on her knees and lets her head fall. She stares down at the palms of her hands and asks, "How...? How did you even get in here?"

I scan the room watching the restless beasts. I really don't want to admit that what I thought was an awesome dream turned out to be a sick trick. My fists are shaking. I look over my mom's shoulder at the queen who is staring back at me. She smiles with a longing behind her eyes and moves to get closer to me. The hollow man shadows her as all the creatures inch forward like a ravenous pack of dogs waiting for Queen Nara's command to attack.

Mom uses her last bit of strength to push off the floor and stands facing me. It's like she flipped a switch and is now completely focused on getting us the heck out of here. Mom starts sputtering orders, "My portal is still open. It will take you straight home." She pulls her cell phone out of her pocket and slips it into mine. "I need you to give this to your dad." She falls forward, catching herself on my shoulders.

I lean forward and check to see if her pupils are dilated. She must have hit her head pretty hard because apparently she wants to get *me* out of here while *she* hangs back to slay the entire Army of Darkness, single handedly. She's crazy if she thinks I'm leaving her like this. "You give it to him. I'm not going anywhere without you." I reach into my pocket to get her cell, but she grabs my arm.

Mom's eyes smile as she says, "I know you'd never leave me." She wraps her arms around my neck and squeezes. Then she whispers, "But sometimes we *have* to do things even when we don't want to."

She pulls back and looks at me. The smile in her eyes fades behind a wave of sorrow as if saying good-bye. Heat swells behind me. An unexpected jolt from my Mom's hands hits my shoulders and knocks me backward into a warm, glowing light.

She drops her chin and gives me that look as if I've just walked in ten minutes after curfew. Her eyes are fixed on mine as she commands, "You *have* to go!"

I try to fight against the portal's current, grasping for anything to hold onto. It feels like I'm swimming against a tsunami forcing unwanted water into my lungs. I ignore the pain and keep fighting. My fingertips are only inches from her arm. Then one of the creatures crawls up behind my mom like a starving bobcat about to pounce on its first meal. Horror flashes across my face.

Mom mouths, "I love you" and nods as if she knows what's coming.

I suck in a breath, but before I can scream, it grabs my mom's feet and slams her face-first into the floor, dragging her away unconscious.

The portal's power overtakes me and flashes like a blue strobe light.

My back hits the wooden floor in our entryway. I can't see anymore, but I hear the queen's voice quake, "Go! Bring *my* son back to me!"

The Army of Darkness is unleashed.

○∞∞○

The impact slides my body across the floor, slamming my head into the wall. The portal is closing. I know her army is right behind me, but I don't care. I jump up in full fight mode and twist to see the light inside the closet flash one last time. The suction of the portal closing slams the door shut. Without a second thought, I run and grab the handle.

I know I shouldn't, but since when has that stopped me? I open the closet.

It's completely dark inside. My stomach clenches into a fist, ready for a fight as I flip the light on.

I push our jackets out of the way. The wall is still there, no light portals, orbs, or crazy-eyed beasts.

My head drops.

No Mom.

My mind races through everything that just happened. I hit the back of the closet wall hoping to find a magic portal button or something to make it open back up. My chest heaves. Too much oxygen floods into my system way too fast. Everything starts spinning around me. I grab the wall and bury my head in my arm. Why didn't she come with me? I force my breaths to slow down and push myself back up. Visions of the beasts flash in my head. The queen's last words send a chill down my spine. Why did she call me *her* son?

I shake my head. This can't be real.

My pocket vibrates. Okay, maybe it is.

I shut the closet and run to get my dad.

Their bedroom door is wide open. I stumble into the doorway, but stop midstride. My dad's sound asleep, lying *next* to Mom.

I stop and grab both sides of the doorframe.

I just saw them kidnap her. My brain's on complete overload.

Dad rolls over and looks at me with groggy eyes. "What's wrong Johnny?"

I let go and back out of their room hoping to avoid an interrogation. Too late.

Dad calls out to me. "Johnny?"

I stand in the hall with my back against the wall. What am I supposed to say? Hey, Dad, I know Mom is lying right next to you, but she just got kidnapped.

I hear my dad turn to my mom. "Maranda. Maranda. Wake up, honey. Something's wrong with Johnny. Maranda."

She isn't responding.

Mom's cell phone is still in my hand. I slide the screen open and look down to see a video waiting. With one touch, I watch my mom's message to my dad.

"David, Nara knows where Johnny is, but I know where she is. I can slow her down and give you time to relocate, but you have to move now. I'm sorry for leaving without you, but there's no time. You know we have to stop her from finding the twelfth descendant or Shamayim will fall." Mom pauses, her eyes filling up with tears. "Sweetheart, you know how to find me if I do not return. I love you, both of you." She blows a kiss toward the camera right before she stops the recording.

I step back into my parents' bedroom and lay the streaming video on the pillow next to my dad who's now sitting up holding Mom's wrist to check her pulse and putting his ear to her chest. Dad glances at the video as he keeps trying to wake her. He grabs her shoulders and shakes her, but her eyes remain still. The only thing moving is her chest, slowly rising and sinking as she labors to breathe.

The recording of my mom's sweet voice chokes him.

She's gone.

Dad looks at me. "Call the ambulance. We've got to get her out of here."

He opens a drawer and starts throwing her things into a bag.

I dial 911. "Dad, what did she mean you know where she is?"

"Johnny, there's no time to discuss this." He goes over to Mom and checks her pulse again and kisses her lips. "Come back to me, sweetheart."

Dad grabs another bag to pack his stuff. I sit down on the bed and run my fingers through Mom's hair and around her face like she does when I'm sick. Do you know I'm here, Mom? I kiss her on the forehead and whisper, "I will find you."

The paramedics come in like they own the place and shove me off to the side. I fold my arms over my stomach and back up until the wall stops me. They load her onto a gurney and tell my dad to follow the ambulance. He's already packed three bags of our clothes when I realize he forgot to get

Mom's makeup. One thing I'm sure of, Mom can't survive without her face paint. What girl can? I run into her bathroom and open the cabinet. Dad walks in behind me as I'm cramming a bag full of her things off of the counter.

"Johnny, we've got to go."

"Just a sec, you forgot Mom's stuff." I zip the bag and start on another pocket.

He grabs my arm, knocking her hair dryer onto the floor, "There's no time!"

I sling his hand off. "There is time! Why are we running away?"

"We're not running away. We're following protocol!" He picks up the dryer and drags me out of the bathroom.

"Whose protocol? I heard Mom tell you to come get her."

His shoulders drop. "Johnny, she knows what she's doing and so do I. You have to trust us."

"Dad, I'm not a kid anymore. Let me help you!"

He picks up a bag and shoves it into my arms. I frown. That's not what I meant. Then he grabs the other two and charges out the door. We hop into the truck, and I refuse to drop the subject.

"How can you just sit here and do nothing when you know how to get Mom back!" I cross my arms and stare out the window.

Dad rubs his neck and puts his hands back on the steering wheel at ten and two. "Johnny, it's not that simple."

"I heard what she said, Dad. You know where she is. So why are we still discussing it? Let's go get her!"

Dad sighs. "It's too dangerous."

"Dangerous for who?"

He glances over at me. "You." He speeds up and runs through a yellow light.

"What's that supposed to mean?"

"Your mom is protecting you. I am protecting you. Don't you think I want to run after her?" He starts rubbing his head again. I've never seen my dad look so defeated.

This is so ridiculous! "Why do you still act like you're the only one who can protect me? I'm old enough to take care of myself!" I sit up tall and look right at him. "Don't you trust me?"

He huffs, "Johnny, it's not about trust. It's my job to protect *you* above all else."

This conversation is pointless. It's like my dad believes a serial killer is after me. I cross my arms and stare out of the window, watching the yellow dashes on the road until I swear they jump off of the pavement, unifying into one solid line of yellow whizzing past my eyes. An eerie silence crowds around me like an angry mob laughing as my brain seizes up, hypnotizing me against my will.

∾⤳∿

I'm standing in the middle of the highway. In slow motion, a black Camaro whirls past me. He's so close that if I wanted to, I could reach out and peel off his white racing stripes. My vision locks on the eyes of the huge man behind the wheel. Two solid-black corneas deepen the emptiness in his vacant orbs. The color of his skin fades into piles of ash from the bottom of an old ashtray. With his arms robotically placed on the steering wheel, he doesn't budge an inch except for the blood draining from his neck. Something big has taken a bite out of that guy and he's dying, or maybe he's already dead. I see movement from the backseat. The man's predator is still inside the Camaro.

The outline of a dark diamond-shaped head with sleek human shoulders forms behind the driver. It slowly hovers around him with serpentine movements. The dark being looks up at me with her familiar vaporous eyes and flashes a victorious smirk, revealing her razor sharp teeth as she whispers deep into the man's ear.

The driver understands his orders and doesn't hesitate to obey his seductress. He jerks the wheel, causing the car to spin completely around. The Camaro's tires skid against the pavement, slamming the car to a complete stop, facing me.

The engine revs with a deep, low rumble. My breathing rate triples as I brace for impact. I'm the deer in the headlights with nowhere to run. The Camaro burns out, fully engaging the 426-horsepower engine and whomping to 61 miles per hour in 5.1 seconds. With my eyes wide open, I watch the howling tires hurl the Camaro straight for me.

ᏃᏋᏃ

I'm sharply ripped out of the vision, like when you dream you're falling and suddenly jump up. I leap in my seat and grab the handle on the truck door, gasping for air.

My dad asks, "You okay?"

Before I can answer, a black Camaro with white racing stripes cuts us off right before the entrance to the hospital. Dad slams on the brakes, causing my seatbelt to jerk me back against the seat. The Camaro passes by my window. I stare at the driver. Two solid black corneas deepen the emptiness in his vacant orbs. The huge man lifts his finger and points directly at me, then he brings his hand to his neck and acts like he's slitting his throat.

I press my lips together and take a deep breath. I wonder if serial killers drive black Camaros? "Dad, no matter what's after me, we still have to bring

Mom back." I watch the Camaro's taillights disappear over a hill.

Dad waits for a safe clearing to turn. "You're right."

I jerk my face to look at him. Is he serious?

He thinks out loud while moving his hand back and forth over the steering wheel. "If you stay with Mom at the hospital, I can go get her and bring her back to her body. Since they don't know where you are, you should be safe."

I guess Dad didn't see the guy driving the Camaro. I'm pretty sure *they* know where I am. My back straightens up. "Uh, no, I'm going with you."

Dad's gives me the fatherly glare, including the twitching eye. "No! You will not go with me."

"Why!"

He jerks the truck across two lanes and into the hospital parking lot. "Johnny, don't you understand? This is all about you. Protect the twelve."

I glare into my dad's eyes. "No, I don't understand! I'm not afraid of the dark, Dad. You and Mom didn't teach me how to fight so that I could hide from the battle."

"Johnny, we've been over this a million times, you aren't old enough."

"And *you* always say I'm the best warrior you've ever seen. So quit hiding the truth from me and tell me, what exactly are we protecting the twelve from?"

Dad's voice is low. "Johnny, I need you to trust me. I promise when I get back, I'll explain everything, but right now, your mom needs me."

My glare relaxes. He's right. Every minute we waste arguing, my mom suffers. "Okay, Dad, but if you're not back in twenty-four hours, I'm coming after both of you."

Dad smiles. "I would expect nothing less, but promise me you won't."

I stare at the floorboard and nod with my fingers crossed. He pulls up to the emergency room and I open my door.

"Johnny."

I turn back to face him, hoping he's changed his mind. "What, Dad?"

"I love you."

I drop my head. "You too."

I grab our bags and walk into the hospital. This is not right. I turn back to watch Dad drive away, but he pulls into a parking spot. I stand up tall and stare. Maybe he changed his mind? I drop our bags and jog back out the double doors just in time to see the blue light of a spirit portal flash inside his truck like a firework with no sound. My shoulders drop.

He's gone.

TO ANOTHER HOME

ANGER MANIFESTS INSIDE of me. I don't think I can control it this time. I didn't ask to be here, and I have no problem being kicked out of another crappy home. My foster brother, JC, and the neighborhood punk, Miguel, pick the wrong time and the wrong place.

"Where do you think you're going?" JC yells out to our foster brother, Jeremy, who keeps his head down and walks faster.

"Hey, punk, I don't remember giving you permission to walk on *my* sidewalk."

I watch JC grab Jeremy and shove him against the apartment building next door.

"Look at him, Miguel, he's such a weak little freak!" They burst into laughter.

My clenched fists are begging to be released. Here we go again. With a deep sigh, I charge straight toward them. Neither dimwit notices. I swear, these two are so stupid that one day they're gonna get run over by a parked car.

JC draws his arm back and swings fast. His fist makes impact right below Jeremy's left ribcage. Jeremy slumps down, but Miguel holds him up for JC to use as a human punching bag.

Time to take out the trash.

I lower my right shoulder and plow into JC as if he's a running back and I'm a lineman hitting him low and hard. He falls into Miguel. Two for one!

I yell to Jeremy, "run!"

I then grab Miguel in a headlock and start punching. Miguel kicks back and strains to over-power me. I move into a choke hold, giving him no room to fight back.

Mr. Rawdon, my foster dad, bursts out the back door of our house and runs across the open lot with Jeremy hovering right behind him. Within seconds, he's pulling me off of Miguel. A trail of blood is dripping from Miguel's nose to his chin, and his eye is already swelling.

JC appears out of nowhere and doesn't waste any time before accusing me of the attack. "I—I was trying to get Johnny to calm down, sir, but he said he hates Mexicans and jumped on top of Miguel. I had to stop him." My eyes tightly focus in on the liar, and I push my sleeves up, ready to finish this.

With a cocky smile, JC looks at Jeremy. "I mean, *we* had to stop him. Right, Jeremy?"

Jeremy grabs his ribs and drops his eyes to the ground. Then he nods his head. You've got to be kidding me! I glare at JC and crack my knuckles.

Mr. Rawdon believes every word. His eyes are small, and his lips press into a thin line showing his teeth as he barks at me, "Get your lousy butt to the house and don't stop until you're in your room!" He turns away to help Miguel up off of the ground.

I stand there with wide eyes. For a split second, my breathing stops. How did JC just get away with lying like that? If I didn't hate him so much, I would ask for lessons.

"*Now*, Johnny!" I haven't seen Mr. Rawdon this mad since JC set the cat on fire and blamed Jeremy. I stomp inside the house and storm past Mrs. Rawdon while she's washing the dishes.

She demands, "Stop right there, young man!"

I was just commanded *not* to stop by Mr. Rawdon. So, I don't. I keep moving and refuse to respond to her. She yells another warning, but I don't care. She's not my mom. It's been over a year of these stupid foster homes, yelling at me and forcing me into counseling. One day I will find my parents and escape the Texas foster system forever. I don't need any of them! I just throw my hands up and fly straight through the kitchen and up to my room.

Mrs. Rawdon's annoying voice chases me down the hallway and up the stairs. Stupid witch! I slam my bedroom door, rattling their family pictures hanging in the hallway, and throw myself on the bottom bunk. My jaw tightens when I hear Mr. Rawdon and his pack of morons invade the kitchen right below me.

Mrs. Rawdon knows the walls in this place are paper thin, but that doesn't stop her mouth. "I'm not surprised Johnny did this. Come here, Miguel, honey, I'll get you some ice."

I stare at the wooden slats on the bunk above me. This is bull crap. I punch the closest board and pull my fist back to rub my aching knuckles. I'm the one who saved Jeremy's face! And this is the thanks I get?

Something moves across the room, I turn my head and see the bedroom door standing wide open.

My arms tighten against my body. What the heck? I just slammed that door.

I lean over and look around the room, but I'm alone.

Maybe I slammed it so hard that it popped back open. I draw a deep breath in through my nose. Whatever. I'm too lazy to get up and shut the door. So I just drop back on my bed and close my eyes.

Footsteps enter my bedroom and approach my bunk. Not. Right. Now. I pretend to be asleep. A cold chill covers my body, making every hair stand on end. Then the bedroom door slams shut. I'm not in the freaking mood! Expecting to see one of my annoying foster brothers, I jerk my head toward the door and punch my fist into the mattress. "What!" I yell out, but no one's there.

My eyes dart all around the room. Maybe there's a draft, or someone shut another door causing this one to slam. Doubt it. I'm sure it's just JC and Miguel trying to get even. "Hilarious, guys, I'm *so* scared. Now get the hell outta here." I throw my pillow at the door and myself back on my bed.

An abnormal silence plays with my mind. I decide to reach for my headphones, but I can't move. My heart jumps. No matter how hard I flex, my arm is stuck to the mattress. My lungs suck in air while every other organ aches under the pressure. An uncontrollable trembling takes over. What. The. Heck. Is. Going. On. My eyes blink over a hundred miles per hour. I can't move, I can't speak, I can't, and then I realize I only have one ability left—sight.

Next to my bed stands a huge man with solid black corneas full of swirling dark fog in his vacant orbs, the Hollow Man. He's staring me down again, but this time we're the only ones in the room—no queen, no Camaro, no Mom. This can't be real. It's just another one of my crazy dreams. I go along for the ride, like I have a choice. The Hollow Man stands there clenching his fists, causing his abnormally large pecs to flex. My heart races, and my stomach threatens to return my lunch. An intense pain surges as he's controlling every cell in my body without touching me.

The Hollow Man speaks, "Prince, why are you lying here as if you are a helpless child?" He turns off his death stare, and I feel an instant release followed by the familiar ache of a four-hour football workout in the Texas heat. Is this guy serious? Prince? And how am I supposed to fight something that isn't really there? My chest tightens, and I try to wake up.

"You are weak. It's time for you to take a stand against those who oppose you."

Weak? I'll show you weak! A surge of adrenaline rushes through my veins. I push off of my bed and jump to my feet. My chest rises, and just as I'm about to open my mouth to give him a piece of my mind, I realize Hollow Man is at least seven feet tall and I'm actually standing just under his armpit. Not a dream!

Maybe I should reconsider my plan of attack.

My senses increase. I hear approaching footsteps. Don't open the door.

The door swings open, I roll my eyes. Idiot.

Then a brain-piercing scream causes my eardrum to consider rupturing. What's Jeremy doing up here? This little punk has caused me enough problems today. I keep my eyes on the Hollow Man and try to control the impulse to attack him as if I'm some kind of superhero.

The Hollow Man looks at me. "Are you going to allow weakness to reign or will you stand up against the traitor?" He points to Jeremy. "Did he not defy the prince?"

Poor kid hovers against the wall as if it can protect him.

For the first time ever, I'm happy to hear Mr. Rawdon's voice, yelling at me as he runs up the stairs to see what's wrong with Jeremy this time. "Johnny, so help me, when I get up there you're gonna be sorry for all the trouble you've started!"

The Hollow Man continues to move toward Jeremy as if he didn't hear the upcoming bulldozer. "Is he not guilty?" the man yells at me with such magnitude that the walls shake. I tremble, not from fear, but anger. Jeremy did throw me under the bus after I saved his sorry butt.

I step toward Jeremy.

I've defended him a million times and without a second thought, he sacrifices me as a worthless scapegoat!

My mind overpowers my heart, making my hands wrap around Jeremy's throat. I know I should stop, but look at all of the trouble I'm in because of *him*.

The Hollow Man laughs in a low growl. "Make him pay for what he has done."

Jeremy grabs my hands. His eyes beg me to let go, but I don't care anymore.

You will pay.

I watch his chest heave up and down, begging for oxygen. A pain strikes my forehead like a knife stabbing into my brain. I squeeze my eyes shut and force my hands to continue making Jeremy suffer.

Deep from within my heart, guilt creeps up my spine. I open my eyes and see the scared little boy at the other end of my hands. I drop him and step back. What am I doing?

The Hollow Man yells, "Finish him!"

I look at Jeremy, lying in a heap of pitiful helplessness. Jeremy's only fault is fear, fear of pain. My anger turns toward the man. "Hey, douche bag, what's your problem?"

Mr. Rawdon thinks I'm talking to him. "What's my problem? You're gonna find out in about two seconds, boy!"

The Hollow Man faces me with a bone-chilling, go-to-hell look. If he doesn't kill me, I'm sure

Mr. Rawdon will. I take my last deep breath and prepare to die.

Within seconds, the Hollow Man lifts off the floor and flies toward me. I brace myself for impact, but his force doesn't stop. Pain takes me to the floor. I collapse under the sudden possession. My lungs squeeze until every oxygen molecule is disintegrated. I can hear the Hollow Man inside my head.

Until you put off all weakness, you will never save anyone.

My chest is at the point of implosion when my foster dad charges into the room, screaming for me to get off of the floor.

The Hollow Man's time is up. He exits through my back, dissolving through the bedroom floor. I heave a deep breath and grab my chest as I roll over and curl into a ball, coughing and gasping for air.

Mr. Rawdon shows no sympathy. He rolls his eyes and asks Jeremy, "What did he do this time?"

A new hurricane of screaming rolls in from downstairs. With my ear to the carpet, I hear what's causing the commotion. The Hollow Man is in the kitchen wreaking havoc. I can't help but chuckle when JC screams louder than the girls.

Mr. Rawdon shoots an angry look at me and yells, "Don't you move, boy!"

Obviously, Mr. Rawdon doesn't understand there's a reason I'm on the floor in the fetal position. He takes Jeremy with him and leaves me there, defenseless.

I hear the girls crying while everyone else is babbling on at the same time.

"Where's it at?" screams a panicked JC. "Is it still chasing me?"

"Someone help Miguel. He can't breathe," cries my oldest foster sister, Rachel. "I think that thing went straight through him. Miguel, focus! Breathe in your nose, out your mouth."

As soon as Mr. Rawdon makes it back downstairs, he orders everyone to calm down. Well, that didn't work. He switches to plan B and screams over the chaos, "Shut up!"

A sudden silence overtakes the house.

The Hollow Man passes through his invisible gateway up through the kitchen ceiling and back into my bedroom. He stands tall and cracks a satisfied smile. "They will think twice before making false accusations about the prince." His eyes meet mine. "Time is running out. Soon you will have to choose a kingdom." He kneels down next to me on the floor and leans in so close that all I can see is his face. "I'm always here, watching, waiting, for you to decide when you are ready to lead the darkness into battle." His head twists and his face distorts, like when you look into a funhouse mirror, until he vanishes into thin air.

My skin is squeezing every muscle against my bones. I need air.

The voices of my scared family members continue to travel up the stairs.

Mrs. Rawdon is spitting words out over a hundred miles per hour. "He's possessed! I've been telling you for weeks that we need to have the priest come for a home visit. What do you have to say now? What? You just saw it. Now is it my overactive imagination?"

Mr. Rawdon isn't exactly supportive. "Actually, I haven't seen a thing except a bunch of screaming kids and my frantic wife. This is ridiculous. What exactly do *you* want me to say to the priest?"

"I don't care what you tell him. Get someone here now or I'm leaving."

"Honey, where do you think you're going to take all of these kids?"

Mr. Rawdon is gonna regret asking her that.

Instead of facing my angry foster parents, I force myself off the floor and sneak downstairs to slip out through the garage before anyone tries to cast anything out of me. I jog down the back alley to the small community park around the corner and scale the metal steps to the tallest slide and sit sideways at the top, hiding under the rusted canopy.

Finally, no more stupid kids, no more screaming adults, and no more hollow guys; I'm all alone. Like a broken record, the last few hours replay incessantly through my mind. That disappearing body builder was frickin' ridiculous! First, he scares the crap out of me and then tells me I'm a weak prince who needs to choose *his* kingdom. I roll my eyes and try to avoid thinking about what I did to Jeremy.

A gust of air blows across my face. I slowly turn my eyes to see what's behind me. Please don't be the body builder. My stomach churns and my muscles stiffen. My eyes dart around, looking for any sign of company. Not weak, huh? I laugh at myself. There's nothing out there but the sky changing from daylight to dusk.

Hiding at the top of this slide is not helping. Life still sucks. I've never been one to back down from a fight, even when it's not mine, but that's exactly what got me in this mess, someone else's problem. I just need to learn to look away and mind my own business. With my head against the cold slide, my eyes close and part of me hopes they won't ever open again.

Everything is pure white, including the grass, the trees, the sky, and even the playground equipment. A black Hummer limousine pulls up from the white street, and a businessman clothed in a black, three-piece suit with a gray-marbled tie steps out from the back. As he walks closer, he calls me by name. I sit up, nearly hitting my head on the slide's rusted canopy to see if I recognize the man, but before I can move, I'm sitting at a nearby picnic table across from him.

My eyes dart around the park. Nothing is moving. Leaves that were falling are suspended in midair. I'm no longer subject to the rules of time on earth. Just being here charges every part of my core. I can't stop the smile as I feel my spirit's power returning. This is my home, the spiritual realm, where everything moves at the speed of light. I take in a deep breath.

The man smiles. "The Queen has a proposition, Prince."

My back stiffens. I stare at the man as he continues to speak.

"On the day that marks the sixteenth year of your birth, you will choose your throne: Prince of Light or Prince of Darkness."

Choose my throne? I look down at my cheap, tattered clothes and laugh. I seriously doubt the prince of the spirit world would be stuck in foster care. My arms cross in front of my chest, and I laugh inside. Funny guy. I hope he doesn't get fired for telling me anything top secret.

"You've been raised to serve the Kingdom of Light where you will reign over a humble but mighty nation."

He flips his hand, making a live video play on the white sky, showing normal people walking next to the Guardians and Celestials on the streets of Shamayim. I take a slow, deep breath. The last time I saw my home, I was a small child. Peace did not exist. The Queen vowed to kill all children until her son was returned to her. So the King ordered the Guardians to move all of the sons and daughters of light to the earth, hiding us among normal, human families, teaching us to blend in until we reach maturity at sixteen years. Only one problem, we are nowhere near normal.

The video pans wide. I see a huge white stone building similar to the Roman Pantheon taking up the horizon. Two blue suns climb high in the sky, illuminating seven thrones.

A bolt of lightning flashes, delivering King Sai to the center throne. His five descendants are right behind him, filling the thrones on each side of him. Except for one. My eyes are fixed on the empty throne at the king's right hand. Something within me wants to sit next to him as if I belong there. I roll my eyes. This guy must be in my head.

The man jumps back to life causing my thoughts to vanish. "But there is an alternative! The Kingdom of Darkness."

A dark feeling swells inside of me as I watch a thick fog cover the suns. A pale moon rises, exposing a mountain covered in waterfalls spilling into a vast, dark ocean. My inner core is rolling. It feels wrong to turn away from the light, but part of me wants to see the other side.

"It's a proud and fierce nation," he narrates as the video hovers over the highest peak, zooming in on an enormous oak tree. Its canopy covers the entire east side of the mountain with water flowing down its leaves and crashing onto a group of boulders. The camera flies toward the tree and nosedives inside. My stomach drops.

Every tree branch is glowing bright enough to light up the entire city hidden below its canopy. There are rows and rows of shops, bars, and restaurants with people scattered everywhere, living life on full-throttled desire. My brain scrambles to explain why this can't be true. Darkness is full of evil, murderous people, but these people are eating, drinking, laughing, and dancing without a care in the world. My heart speeds up. The so-called truth is shattering before my eyes. What if the Guardians haven't been protecting me from the dark, they're keeping me away from it?

The man interrupts again. "The queen is prepared to offer you all the riches in this world."

As he speaks, the sky turns into piles of green cash. He has my complete attention.

"All the power in this world."

Underneath me, the bench moves. I grab for anything to help balance myself. Chair arms and black velvet cushions stretch up and out to form a massive throne around me. Then the ground starts rumbling and cracking. The grass below me peels away from the earth and levitates, rising ever higher into the sky. My stomach begs me to squeeze my eyes shut, but a roller-coaster adrenaline rush, like when you're waiting to fly down the tallest hill forces me to keep my eyes wide open. I hold on to the arms of my new throne chair and lean over to watch every blade of grass and speck of dirt fly away, exposing a magnificent platform driving me upward. I watch as we climb higher and higher into the air overlooking the park, overlooking the city, overlooking the entire earth.

The man in black smiles and points below. "And all the glory in this world."

Thousands of people from earth are climbing a million golden stairs passing through the clouds to reach my throne. They don't stop until they see me. Then they start screaming and trying to grab any part of me like crazy fans trying to touch the lead singer on stage at a concert. I feel invincible! The cheering turns into a contagious roar. People are jumping up and down, holding their arms in the air, screaming my name, "Johnny, Johnny," over and over. Warmth radiates throughout my body, justifying all of the sacrifices that led up to this moment. If only this were real.

The man in black is standing on the platform next to me. He raises his arms as if he's a game show host displaying the grand prize. "You will be the highest and mightiest man alive! Anyone who has wronged you will be brought to *your* justice." Flashes of past foster parents, teachers, and thugs like JC flash through my mind. My teeth grind together. One day we will meet again, and I will not be the one cowering.

The man in black leans over my shoulder. "Think about it. The whole world will be at your fingertips, as it should be."

I look out over the vast horizon, listening to the cheers all around me. This is impossible. A slow smile spreads across my face.

The man's eyes thin out and his spine relaxes. "Prince Johnathon, this is your birthright, and it is a disgrace for you to continue in such humble surroundings."

He snaps. Everything returns to white. My body drops through the air as if gravity is angry, slamming me back onto the picnic bench. I scowl at the man, but he smirks as if he just successfully completed his favorite trick. I shake my head. This guy has definitely dropped out of the sky one too many times.

He takes a quick breath and rambles on, "Regardless of kingdom, the people on earth will bow to your throne."

He diverts my attention to the video, which is now split into two scenes. On one side, the blue suns are shining on a newborn lamb lying on the seat of a throne with an endless crowd of outcasts kneeling before the footstool. The other side is a grand ballroom full of wealthy constituents standing before a golden throne with two roaring lions pacing and watching for someone to devour.

Good thing I'm not the prince: I want both worlds.

The man reaches in his coat pocket and hands me a cell phone with an active countdown: fifty-six days, six hours, six minutes, and fifty-six seconds. We are back in the human dimension under their rules of time. I get lost watching the seconds count backward one by one. It feels like a million ants are crawling throughout my body. I know who my parents are, and they're not the rulers of the spirit world. The man's voice growls, making my stomach turn as he speaks. "I'll see you soon." When I jerk my eyes up, he's gone and everything is completely blacked out.

∞

Flashing lights flicker behind my closed eyelids. I stretch and rub my eyes, trying to focus. Boy am I surprised to see the chubby face of a middle-aged man pop up in front of me and order, "It's time to get up, Johnny. You need to come with me." Now I'm sure that police car by the curb is waiting for *me*. Not what I was expecting.

Next thing I know, I'm sitting on the couch in the Rawdon home, listening to the police officer give me a long lecture. Then, in walks Ms. Sara, my case manager from Child Protective Services. She's a tall, beautiful lady with long, blond hair, looking hot as ever. Usually she's pretty nice, but not today.

Her brow's crumpled as she walks over to me. "Johnny, you finally quit trying to run away and now you're attacking people! What's going on with you?"

I shrug my shoulders and stare at the floor, refusing to look up at her. Every time I get in trouble, her eyes make me feel like the inside of my soul is being x-rayed. So I've learned to avoid eye contact at all costs.

My foster mom brings out my eviction notice, a large blue duffel bag. I guess since the priest is a no-show, it's time for me to hit the road. Even though I want to leave, I'll never get used to being kicked out. I take my bag from Mrs. Rawdon, who refuses to look me in the eye. This is not right. My whole life I've been taught to stand up for the weak and look where that's gotten me. Being the hero isn't all it's cracked up to be.

Lesson learned.

SOMETHING'S DIFFERENT

"WE'RE GETTING CLOSE, Johnny. Are you doing all right back there?" asks Ms. Sara.

I can't stop the sarcastic tone in my voice, "Just great."

From the looks of things, this place gets worse with every mile down this highway to redneck hell! We turn off the main road and curve through a forest of trees and bounce over two gigantic ruts full of muddy water. Ms. Sara veers the car down a half-dirt, half-rock horseshoe driveway. These people can't even afford cement. The sun slips through the tops of the trees, casting a spotlight on my new foster home. Set back in the woods sits a huge, two-story brick house.

I love it, but I hate it.

The front door opens, and my new foster mom appears. She has brown highlighted hair that sits on her shoulders and frames her bright, ocean blue eyes. I grab my blue duffel and follow Ms. Sara inside.

She introduces us. "Johnny, this is Mrs. Johnson."

With the sweetest smile, the lady replies, "You can call me Susan."

I try to smile as I nod at her.

She takes my bag and sits it down on the desk chair by the bookshelves.

Susan turns back to face me. "You've had a long day. I bet you're ready for things to settle down."

Again, all I do is nod. She doesn't seem to mind my lack of words.

Susan pats my shoulder and says, "Things will only get better from here." She smiles. "Make yourself at home. Ms. Sara and I will be around the corner in the kitchen."

They walk out of the room and leave me standing there. Never has a new foster parent done that! Usually, they eyeball me, acting like I might steal something or put their house dog in the dryer. This is a good sign. I look around at the family photos hanging on the walls. In every picture, there's a different set of kids except for the same blond boy and girl who I assume are twins.

A delicious smell makes my mouth water. As if on cue, my stomach growls. If this were my house, I would have already run into the kitchen and lifted a free sample when Mom wasn't looking.

Something crashes in the kitchen. A young boy's voice floats in the air, "Sorry."

Then a loud engine rattles the walls. Someone yells, "Dad's home!" My heart pounds. I move to a chair in the corner, fidgeting with a string hanging off the bottom of my shirt. The door opens. Mr. Johnson is a giant with a long, red goatee, bald head, and tattoos everywhere! Confidently, he strides into the living room.

"Is there something new in here?" asks Mr. Johnson.

I force a smile.

"Oh, Dad, it's Johnny." A blond girl bounces into the room and smiles at me. "Hi, I'm Caylee."

Immediately, I recognize her and the guy walking in behind her.

He nods. "I'm Canyon."

No mistake about it, they're twins.

Then the young boy yells from behind the couch, "I'm Marcos." All I see is a pudgy little hand fly up into the air and wave.

"My name is Valerie," a pretty young girl appears from behind the couch, giggles, and disappears again.

Then I see a girl with long dark curls walk down the stairs. She lifts her head slightly and looks straight at me. Time stands completely still as she smiles, which gives me enough time to catch a glimpse of her icy blue eyes right before she looks down at the floor. I think I'm in love.

Mr. Johnson says, "I'm Ray, and that over there's Danielle."

He sticks out his huge right hand, slicing through my vision of Danielle. I stretch out my arm and give a firm shake just like my dad taught me. His grasp in return is strong, his arm tough.

We make eye contact, and he smiles back at me. "No need to worry anymore, I've got your back."

He drops my hand and goes into the kitchen. "Something smells good in here!"

I don't move.

Everyone piles into the dining room, taking their places and filling their plates. Caylee walks over to me and sticks her hand in front of my face, palm up.

"Come on, Johnny. I promise you'll like us." She may have used nice words, but her tone is quite sarcastic. Caylee grabs my hand to pull me up whether I want to or not. She pulls so hard that we stumble into each other and almost hit the floor.

"Thanks." I roll my eyes.

She catches the sarcasm and tosses some of her own right back, "Anytime, *little* brother."

She leads the way into the dining room and sits across from me. Marcos is next to me and keeps his head down, eating quietly, but every now and then I catch a smile quickly lost behind a napkin. His sister is quite the opposite, Valerie asks me a different question every five seconds.

"Johnny, when's your birthday? How old are you?"

"February twenty-ninth and I'll be sixteen."

Valerie says a little too loud, "That's cool! Do you get a party on the years that skip your birthday?"

"Yes, on the twenty-eighth, but this year is a leap year."

"Let's have a big party!" She hits Danielle under the table and giggles. Then she continues the interrogation, "What grade are you in?"

"Ninth."

Valerie doesn't smile and looks to Danielle who looks equally disappointed. I laugh. "Just kidding, I'm in tenth grade." Their smiles return along with more questions.

"Do you have a girlfriend?"

Danielle almost chokes on her food and bugs her eyes out at Valerie, but Valerie doesn't seem to care. She wants an answer. Good thing I don't have anything to hide around this girl, she's one tough mama. "No girlfriend, why do you ask? Don't tell me you date older guys."

Valerie giggles and looks down. For the first time, she's speechless.

⟨∞⟩

Once everyone finishes eating, they hop up and start cleaning. Awkward. Everyone knows exactly what his or her job is, as if working in a well-organized restaurant, except for me.

Then Danielle asks, "You wanna go outside?"

"Sure." I feel my face flush.

Valerie chimes in, "I'll get my shoes and meet you out there."

Danielle shrugs her shoulders as we walk out the back door.

I start off the conversation, "So, what's your story?"

"You're not bashful, huh?" She smiles and walks over to lean on the porch rail.

I smile and state the obvious, "I don't like to waste time."

Danielle laughs at me and drops her eyes to the wood deck. I press for an answer, "Seriously, why are you here?"

She looks up. "The Johnsons are my aunt and uncle. I'm just staying here until my parents come back."

I nod my head. "Where'd they go?"

She looks down at the ground and mumbles "That's what I'd like to know."

My brow crumples. "You seriously don't know where they went?"

Danielle shakes her head.

I try not to stutter, "How long have they been gone?"

She shifts from one foot to another. "About eight months." Her eyes fill with tears. She stiffens her back and changes the subject, "So, what about you?"

I clear my throat. "Well, my mom's in a coma and my dad disappeared."

Her eyes widen. "What do you mean disappeared?"

Our eyes connect. I'm the only person here who understands what it's like to lose both parents. She needs me, I can feel it. I want to tell her more, but I hesitate. Then the back door pops open and a herd of kids push out the door, screaming, "You're it!"

I feel someone slap me on the arm. Danielle looks at me like I have the plague and runs. At first, I stand there in shock. I haven't played tag since like sixth grade and they think I'll be it? Everyone's running away from me except Caylee. Here comes the sarcasm.

"It's okay if you don't want to be it. I understand being scared in a new place."

That's all she had to say, *scared*. Me, scared? Whatever! I leap toward her and tag her on the arm, yelling, "You're it!"

Caylee swings her arm around so fast that I didn't even see it coming. It lands right on my leg as she runs off, yelling, "Noooo, *you're* it!"

Game on.

෬᩠ᩮᩣ

After a few rounds, Ms. Sara walks outside and catches me. "I'm about to leave. Can we talk for a sec?"

I sit beside her on the porch swing and watch the kids run back and forth.

"So, how are you feeling?"

"Pretty good." In reality, I'm ecstatic, but I play it cool.

"I'm so glad," her eyes twinkle as if to say *I told you so.* "Well, is there anything you need before I go?"

I lower my voice and simply reply with a confident, "Nope."

She quickly answers, "Good. I couldn't leave you if I thought you weren't happy." A huge smile spreads across her face. "I'll be back to check on you in a week or so."

Ms. Sara has always protected me. I jerk my head sideways to swing my hair back over my eyebrow and allow one tiny smile. "Thanks." There's so much more I want to say, but the words refuse to come out.

AT MY NEW SCHOOL

THE SUN'S UP. I pull the blanket over my head and try to fall back asleep. I'm not ready for this, again. I hate new schools.

Susan's voice ruins my plan to stay under cover. "Everyone up."

Canyon slides down off the top bunk and grabs his clothes. "How'd you sleep?"

"Fine, I guess." Actually, I don't remember a thing. Why don't I remember anything? My head begins to pound.

"You must have been dreaming some crazy stuff." Canyon chuckles.

"Why do you say that?" I try to act normal and grab my clothes, hoping I didn't try to attack him last night. If they find out about my dreams, I'm sure I'll be gone by bedtime. Another foster home bites the dust. I drag myself across the room, preparing for the worst.

Canyon harasses me, "You talk more in your sleep than you do when you're awake."

I press my lips together. I'm not sure what to say. I don't need any more problems.

Canyon must be able to see the stress on my face. "Don't worry, I don't plan on telling anyone." He pauses and tilts his head. "Unless…"

Here's the catch, another foster brother threatening to turn me in for what my alter ego does in the midnight hour unless I do his homework or chores or something stupid like that. Time to see what he wants for his silence. "Unless what?"

"Unless you start sleepwalking naked. That's definitely a deal breaker." He slugs my arm and laughs.

I stare at him, waiting for the terms of blackmail, but he just keeps laughing. I nod and laugh off his comment, but seriously wonder what he heard and what he plans to do about it. Normally I remember my dreams, or at least part of them, but not last night. This can't be good. Maybe the counselors are right, my "pent-up anger" and "suppressed memories" are getting to me.

⟨∽∽⟩

The drive to school is way too short. After we drop off the younger two kids, Susan parks in her designated spot on the east side of the building. The last three kids pile out of the car, running in different directions for athletics, tutoring, or waiting in the commons area with the rest of the high school minions. Not me. My stomach churns as I turn the other way to follow Susan through the side door and down a hall into my new torture chamber, aka the front office. The room is small and completely empty.

A blond lady with happy eyes pops up from behind the front desk. "Well, here he is! Johnny, I've heard all about you!"

I jump and drop my notebook, scattering pencils across the floor.

Susan laughs and grabs a couple of pencils that rolled next to her feet. "Johnny, I'd like you to meet our favorite secretary, Mrs. Martinez."

I nod at her with a tiny smile, secretly wishing she'd disappear again.

The lady primps her hair dramatically. "Yes, there's none like me." After a slight laugh, she straightens up and looks me in the eye. "Now, Johnny, if you need any help or get lost or hungry, you come find me. I take care of all the Johnson kids." She covers one side of her mouth to block Susan from seeing. "Someone has to."

Susan nudges me with her elbow. "She does homework too."

They both laugh as if it's an inside joke. I smile, but seriously wonder if I can get her to do my homework. I'd be willing to pay if she's good at math!

Mrs. Martinez hands me a piece of paper. "Here's your schedule. If you'll hold on a sec, I'll get a student to help you find your locker and show you around."

I know a certain girl that I've been trying to talk to ever since I moved here sitting in commons right now. Considering all the other Johnson kids are too busy to interrupt, this will be the perfect opportunity to actually get to talk to her, *alone*. I try to act cool and suggest, "I think Danielle's sitting in the commons."

Mrs. Martinez takes the bait. "Great idea. I'll go get her."

Score! I lean against the wall and read over my schedule, trying to act cool.

Boggs, Johnathan D.

Term	Period	Class	Room	Teacher	Credits
2	1	Athletics	GYM	Garcia	0.000
2	2	W History	103	Brooks	0.000
2	3	Chemistry	101	London	0.000
2	4	Tech	204	Duncan	0.000
2	5	English I	304	Chaffin	0.000
2	6	STAAR	304	Chaffin	0.000
2	7	T Leader	407	Lilley	0.000
2	8	Algebra I	311	Peters	0.000

Eight classes a day. Well, that's better than ten at my last school. I hate double block schedules. I guess some schools think if they cram more information into us per hour we will learn more. I don't think so. My brain shuts down after ten minutes. Period.

Susan walks up next to me. "You need anything else before I go to work?"

I shake my head.

"Okay, then. Have a good day."

She leaves the office as Danielle walks in with an obvious smirk and grabs my schedule out of my hand. "Follow me."

Before I can turn around, Danielle has come and gone. I chase her out of the office and around the corner. She stops in the first hall and dramatically swings both arms like an airline stewardess to point at my locker. "Here's your locker. You might want to keep stuff in it. The rest of this place is called the one hundred hall where your history and chemistry classes are. Then you walk to the next hallway and it's the *two hundred hall*. Imagine that." She tilts her head and hip with such attitude that it's adorable.

She pauses for a moment and I jump on the opportunity to gain some brownie points. "You know, you're the finest tour guide in town, which is why I requested you personally."

She blushes and tries to ignore me as she sticks her arm out to point down the two hundred hall. "That's your technology class and across the hall is Susan's classroom, just in case you get a boo-boo or need a safe place full of balls."

I tilt my head and ask, "Full of what?"

She smiles for real this time. "She has exercise balls for chairs. Pretty cool if you ask me."

"Do the other classes have balls?" After the words leave my lips, I realize how it sounds. I wait to see Danielle's response, preparing for more attitude.

"Nope, she's the only teacher with balls." There's an awkward silence followed by an eruption of laughter. She waves for me to follow her as we head to the three hundred hall. "English and Algebra are down there. Now your Teen Leadership class will be on the other side of the school. Do I need

ONE PRINCE, TWO KINGDOMS

to show you where that is too or can you figure that one out on your own?"

"I think I got it covered. You're such an excellent tour guide but don't quit your day job." There's that cute attitude again.

"Not a problem. Now you better get to the field house. Practice started five minutes ago."

I'm late.

Football is a slam, *literally*, but Canyon promises to teach me some plays at home. Something's got to help keep my feet on the turf. I follow the team into the field house with my helmet under my arm. Of course, there isn't enough time for a real shower, so I rinse off and take a quick cologne shower. The bell rings, sending a stampede of footballers into the halls. I make it to my locker, but it's already a complete ghost town. Not good.

I slide inside Ms. London's science class just as the tardy bell screams overhead. I stand by the white board, making it very obvious that I'm the awkward new kid. The silence in her classroom freaks me out as if a monster is lurking in the supply closet waiting to devour the first person who makes a sound. The quiet teenagers walk past me to their assigned desks, place their books under their seats, and then uniformly place their arms on top of their desks. I just entered the Twilight Zone. I shift from side to side, wishing I could run, but it's too late.

A deep, raspy voice clangs in my ear from behind me. "What are you doing in here, young man?"

I turn and see an older woman with black-and-gray hair. She has a large face with wild eyes. Fear goes down my spine, and I can't speak.

"Excuse me, but I need an answer. Now!" she barks at me.

I stutter, "J—Johnny Boggs, ma'am. I'm new."

"Oh. Right," she huffs. "Just sit there," Ms. London commands as she points her long, boney finger to a desk in the far right corner.

Her magic words push me, causing a slight stumble as I scramble to get to my assigned desk. It feels like I'm turning my back on the enemy, expecting a bullet to tear through my spine at any moment. I hurry past all the students, glancing from one soulless face to another. What has this lady done to these kids? Just as I'm about to lose all hope, I meet a pair of familiar eyes with life still inside, Danielle.

Her hotness electrocutes me, melting every bit of common sense. Her brilliant blue eyes, full pink lips, and dark curls make me smile. Take a breath, Johnny. I sit down and force my thoughts to focus on the teacher's boring, outdated PowerPoint presentation about the periodic table. She probably knows it by heart from her potions. My thoughts drift back to Danielle. I turn and stare at her, leaning my head on my hand. We aren't related, and she's not an official foster sister. She's just a visiting foster cousin. I shake my head. No way, it's too awkward. This is an official friend zone. I turn back to face the front and try not to fall asleep from acute boredom.

My eye catches the girl in the second desk two rows over from me. She's completely and perfectly beautiful, like, this-creature-must-have-been-accidentally-dropped-from-heaven beautiful! My lungs constrict. Her hair is golden blond. She's wearing a gray skirt with a pink shirt, and has pulsating green eyes like waves rolling in from the depths of the ocean. My head falls to one side. Then, her expression flips upside down.

Why is she looking at me like that? My goofy grin retreats. Maybe it's because you're still gawking, idiot. I force my eyes to move and slump down in my seat, trying to disappear.

The bell finally frees me from my humiliation. I stand and turn to face Danielle as she picks up her notebook and purse. I try to make small talk. "So is she always this sweet in class?"

Danielle chuckles. "No, she was only that nice because you're the new kid."

I walk with Danielle a few feet behind the hot blond and her friends. They stop in the middle of the hall, creating an instant traffic jam.

Danielle doesn't hold back. "Some people are so rude! As if they own the *entire* hallway."

The girls crowd around one locker, taking turns using the mirror, giving the rest of us just enough room to push around them.

Danielle laughs louder and higher than normal. She grabs my arm, holding her hand there just a little too long, acting like she's a complete airhead. I'm pretty sure she's impersonating the hot blond and her friends who we are walking around right now. The blond girl's two friends look over their shoulder at us and roll their eyes. I look into their locker mirror. The hot blond stares back at me through the reflection. She smiles. Her eyes move from me to Danielle. Instantly, the blond girl's image flashes to a pale, angry beast, hissing at Danielle with sharp teeth. My stomach drops. I keep staring as she flashes back to a beautiful blond, smiling at me.

My eyes pop. I jerk my head forward, but not before I stumble over nothing.

Danielle grabs my arm and laughs. "You should really watch where you're going."

ONE PRINCE, TWO KINGDOMS

I force myself to laugh with her as I look over my shoulder one more time to see the three hot girls sauntering away.

That did not just happen. I shake it off and run by my locker to get my language arts book. Kids are everywhere like ants after you step on their mound. I shuffle through the halls and hurry to Mr. Chaffin's class in room 304. My nerves are making my stomach turn. I stand there and stare at the classroom door. Surely he can't be worse than Ms. London!

A very large guy comes up behind me. "Are you going in or not?"

I take the hint and open the door to see black walls covered with posters from Broadway plays and musicals. There's even a stage with velvet curtains set up behind his desk. In the center of the room is a table covered with stacks of large pieces of colorful paper and buckets of markers. The students all pour in and put their stuff in a cubbyhole by the door.

I stand back and watch the controlled chaos. Everyone gets to work either creating posters or putting on costumes. How can this be language arts? I must be in the wrong class. I pull out my schedule to check the room number.

A theatrical voice announces from behind the curtain, "Welcome, Mr. Boggs! I have been expecting you!" Then a man with a black goatee and short black hair and wearing a black silk cape hops down off the stage and strides toward me. I know my eyes are huge because I can feel the tension on my face.

"You may call me Maestro. This is your language arts class that will be taught in a most unique way."

Well, that statement blows my wrong class theory out of the water.

He continues speaking at me without taking a breath, "You will learn to perceive the world around you as a theatrical production. Life is theater." The volume and annoying tone of his voice makes me think he's performing for an audience of thousands. "Today's assignment is to create a playbill for your own Broadway production of your life. So grab a color of paper that suits you and begin creating!" He flings his cape back, turns, and struts over to a group of students who are having trouble finding the wig for their upcoming play.

I'm trying to choose a color of paper, when I hear the sweetest hello in my life.

"I guess we have two classes together." I turn and see the gray skirt and pink shirt smiling at me. She looks frickin' amazing up close as long as no one makes her mad.

I try to act cool. "Yep, I guess so." Immediately, I regret using the stupid word *yep*. Dude, try to at least sound halfway intelligent.

"What color are you choosing?" she asks me.

I don't want her to know how badly I'm over-thinking this whole color thing, so I say the first one that comes to mind. "Blue."

She smiles. "Me too. Do you want to work with us?"

"I guess so," I answer. Immediately, I regret saying *I guess so*. Why can't I say what I mean to this girl? She seems to make my mind get all mixed up, and I get so freaking nervous like I'm shooting the final basket to win or lose the game for my team. We grab our blue papers and sit on the floor by three other people.

She sits down gracefully, as if posing to have her portrait painted. "By the way, my name is Shay and that's Mckenzee, Noet, and Ben."

I'm staring again.

Say something, you freak. "Hi." I reach out and then feel stupid so I drop my hand. "I'm Johnny."

She swoops her hair over one shoulder. "Nice to officially meet you."

Throughout the rest of class, I try to focus on my work, but occasionally Shay sweeps her bangs out of her eyes and I'm hypnotized. When I'm near her, I forget where I am. In fact, I forget everything.

☙

Lunch and my afternoon classes are all hazy. The good news—my first day is over. I walk out of Ms. Peters's class with Danielle to her locker, thinking about how much I still hate math.

"How was your day?" Danielle asks.

"It was fine until this stupid homework," I growl.

"It's so easy, what are you whining about?" Her teasing me is so comfortable, as if I've known Danielle since elementary school. We're at her locker, crowded in a mass of student zombies rushing for the bus. One girl bumps into me, knocking me into Danielle. She drops her books and falls into my chest. I feel her breath against my neck. Back up, this is not how a friend zone works. She's so close, I can almost feel her heartbeat. But she's so hot. I don't really care who's looking or what rules we're breaking. I lean in. This is their cousin, not mine.

Olivia, a girl from our math class, breaks the moment. "Hey, D, whatcha doin' after school today?"

I kneel down to pick up Danielle's books while she tries to focus her thoughts.

"I—I, um, I have homework."

Olivia laughs. "Me too. That was kinda the point. Don't you go to Mrs. J's classroom for a while?"

"Yes, but I…" Danielle looks to me for help.

I hand her the books off the floor and jump right in. "She has to go get Marcos and then we're leaving early."

"Oh, right. Well, call me if you can study later."
Olivia smiles mischievously and elbows her, obviously implying a hidden meaning to the word *study*.
Danielle laughs and closes her locker as Olivia runs off, hollering at another girl to wait up.

"What was that all about?" I ask.

"Oh, I don't know. Olivia's always up to something. Thanks for the save." She bumps against my shoulder in a playful way, but my body interprets it much differently. I need to go by my locker, but I choose Danielle over schoolwork. We turn toward the main hallway, and I see a huge problem in a gray skirt walking straight for us. Shay. She's laughing with a group of girls, but the moment she sees me with Danielle, her eyes pierce Danielle as if shooting daggers straight into her heart. Good thing looks aren't lethal. Shay turns her gaze to me, softening instantly as if the sour finally wears off her candy.

"Hi, Johnny, whatcha doing after school?" Shay moves close to me.

Once again, my words don't cooperate. "I don't know."

She grabs a piece of paper off of her friend's binder and writes on it. "Call me. I just live around the corner from the Johnsons. We should hang out tonight."

She stuffs the paper in my pocket and looks into my eyes for a *long* time. I feel like a love-struck puppy and probably look like one too, complete with the big, stupid grin. Shay seems to like my smile. It literally hurts when she drops our stare and cuts her eyes to Danielle. Her shoes drum the tile floor and her hips sway in rhythm as she walks away. I want to follow her, but with each breath her love potion dilutes and I come back to my senses.

Danielle spouts, "I can't stand that girl."

I look over my shoulder to see if Shay heard her. "Why? She seems pretty nice." I chose the wrong words and Danielle is quick to let me know it.

"Yeah, I hear ya. She seems *pretty*." Danielle rolls her eyes and steps away from me.

"That's not what I meant." I try to backtrack as I hop to catch up to her. We're now at Susan's door. I stop in front of Danielle so she has to answer me. "Seriously, what makes you hate her?"

Danielle unleashes on me. "She's a fraud! Fake hair, fake nails, fake smile. How can you believe anything she says? I bet she's hideous first thing in the morning."

I squint my eyes and act like I'm in deep thought. "I bet you're right. She could be hiding a disgusting beast underneath all that fakeness."

Danielle stares at me. I stare back.

Her face softens. I smile.

Her lips twist into a smirk. I can't hold it back anymore and neither can Danielle. We both laugh right when Canyon opens the classroom door. "What are you two laughing about?"

"Your face." Danielle slugs Canyon in the stomach.

He grunts and slouches. She pushes past him, patting his back to give a little encouragement. I step up, but Canyon isn't about to let me pass. He stands and shoots me a sarcastic smile as if to say *Thanks a lot, bro.* I follow him into Susan's classroom and sit on an exercise ball at the table beside Danielle, trying to focus on math instead of curls and batting eyelashes. Right when I finish the last problem, Susan announces it's time to leave. Score, homework's done before I get home!

UNTIL...

"JOHNNY! JOHNNY!" ALL of the Johnson kids are yelling at me from around the corner. I walk around the house to see all four of them on the trampoline chanting my name. Danielle is standing off to the side.

Canyon yells, "Come on!"

"Uh, are we all going to fit?" I'm not sure that I'm willing to die on a trampoline with four other smelly kids.

"Sure, we do it all the time," hollers Canyon.

"Um, I think I'll watch." I completely trust Canyon when it comes to showing me football plays, but not trampoline stunts. I have seen and felt the damage he can do on the ground. I'm not about to add airtime and three other people to the mix.

I walk over and sit in one of the lawn chairs by the pool. Danielle is not far behind me. Over the last six weeks, we have become inseparable except when I'm with Shay. Of course, that drives Danielle completely crazy, which is part of the fun. If we didn't live together, I would ask Danielle out, but she's the closest thing I have to a best friend since my parents went missing, and I'm not about to lose her. We kick back and watch Marcos fly up like a rocket over five or six feet in the air before he crashes face first into the trampoline. Of course, he blames Valerie and they start screaming.

"Do they ever stop fighting?"

Danielle laughs. "Not since the day they moved in."

The wind picks up, blowing leaves across the yard. Danielle rubs her arms. I think about teasing her for not wearing a jacket, considering January is still considered winter, although in Texas it could be seventy degrees outside today and twenty tomorrow. Instead, I just take off mine and hold it out. She looks up through her bangs, smiles, and takes the offering. Canyon is now showing off his backflips freestyle. I hope he doesn't flip Marcos off the trampoline.

I feel someone staring at me. I turn and catch Danielle's eyes. She looks down at her fingernails and fidgets. I keep staring, enjoying her uneasiness. She peeks up a couple of times and finally says, "So, you were meaning to tell me how your dad disappeared." She definitely knows how to turn the tables. Now I'm looking down at my fingers.

I stutter, "I…I was?"

"Yeah." She pulls her hair over to one side of her face and twists it around her finger. She doesn't even have to try to be beautiful.

I lean back in my chair and smile at her. She's serious. I can tell from her raised eyebrow and folded arms that she's determined to get an answer. I guess I can give her just enough details to make her happy because, honestly, the whole truth sounds completely insane. "Well, my dad told me he was going after something for my mom and left me at the hospital. I stayed next to my mom for three days watching the machines go up and down, waiting for my dad. Next thing I know, CPS shows up and here I am."

"I know exactly what you're talking about." Our eyes lock. There's no way she understands. I just nod and hope she'll drop it, but what girl would?

She looks down at her hands. "My parents work for the government. One night, the department called with orders to go below ground and bring back the missing."

Wait, what? I turn my head and stare at her. Is she seriously talking about the spirit world?

Danielle has my complete attention as she continues, "My parents knew the risk, but they also knew how important it was to stop the disappearances. So my mom called my Aunt Susan to babysit, and here I am, still waiting."

I sit there, motionless. Danielle hides her face from me, a tear slipping down her cheek. I look over at the trampoline to make sure the other kids are still distracted. I put my hand on her knee. "I'm sorry, Danielle. I promise it will be okay."

She pulls her head up and wipes her eye. "How can you say that!"

I crumple my brow. "I don't know, but all of this will work itself out somehow."

"Johnny, I've been waiting long enough for it to *work out*! I want my parents back, my life back! Don't you?" She looks like she might lose it at any second.

I force myself to answer, "Of course I do, Danielle, but sometimes we have to accept that things might not ever be the same."

Danielle's face twists up and she takes a deep breath. Here it comes. "Are you kidding me? My parents go to save your mom and you're just gonna give up!"

My stomach hits the ground. She definitely knows who I am. Danielle starts to yell, but quickly lowers her voice when Caylee looks over at us. Now *my* breathing is out of control, waves of nausea flowing through my stomach. I look down and try to think. How's this possible? Has she known this whole time without saying a word?

I look up and watch Danielle smile and wave at Caylee like everything's hunky-dory. Canyon sneaks up and jumps right next to Caylee, sending her soaring. Danielle laughs. My forehead's throbbing. One minute this girl is yelling at me for giving up and the next, she's laughing. Whiplash.

I squint my eyes at Danielle and whisper with my lips firmly in place, "I will never give up."

Her voice is high and cheerful, "So what's your plan?"

I drop my eyebrows, "What do you mean by that?"

Her head tilts and she gives me a serious but beautiful stare deep into my eyes. "I *mean*, what are *you* going to do about it? Don't try to tell me you haven't thought about going to find them."

My stomach flutters. I can't stay mad at this girl.

"Well, yeah, but how am I supposed to know where they are?" I'm starting to feel like I need to lawyer up.

She leans forward, giving me only a few inches to breathe. "You said your mom is in a coma. Isn't that a big enough clue?"

My knee bounces and I shrug my shoulders.

Danielle sits back and laughs out loud. "You don't know, do you?" Her grief is now in stage two. Anger.

"Don't know what?" I glance to see if the others are looking, but they're too busy flying Canyon up into the trees.

"Tell me that you at least know who you are," she demands.

I stick my hand out. "Johnny Boggs, nice to meet you."

She slaps it away and rolls her eyes, "I'm serious!"

I open my mouth, but nothing comes out. She nods me on like a parent trying to get their toddler to walk for the first time. I lean forward and whisper, "I have no idea what you're getting at."

She glares directly in my eyes. "You've got to be kidding me right now. Seriously, drop the act. I already know *who* you are, Prince."

My brain literally drops to my toes. Every ounce of blood flees from my face. I stare at her, hoping for a grin or a slap on the back to prove she's joking, but her eyes are dead set. She's not budging.

Danielle drops her chin. "Did you really think you were the only person from Shamayim? Open your eyes!" She pauses a moment to let her words sink in.

I watch Caylee fly up in the air as if it's second nature. Canyon is barely using any of his strength to make her soar. How did I not see it before? My eyes jump from person to person.

Danielle continues, "I've been watching you for a while. At first, I thought I was crazy, but you don't cover your royalty very well."

I try to remain calm. "And what do you mean by that?"

"Like what you just did right there. Normal teens would have gotten mad and stomped off or at least said a few explicit words, but not you. Mr. Goody-Two-Shoes always has to be politically correct. And it's funny how you always seem to get out of trouble at school, like when you didn't finish your math homework, but somehow got an A." She tilts her head, quite pleased with her presentation of the evidence.

I don't need to hear anymore. Flashes of the man in black flood my mind. *On the day that marks the sixteenth year of your birth, you will choose your throne, Prince of Light or Prince of Darkness.* His job was to present me with choices, not to convince me of who I am. If she's right, then I'm in real danger. Any Trog or Celestial should be able to spot me a mile away.

I grab my forehead and close my eyes, trying to focus on a plan, but all I can do is flip through memories of my life. Why didn't they tell me? Growing up, feeling like a freak surrounded by normal humans, it would have been nice to know at least one other kid like me. Dad said he would explain everything when he gets back. But will he ever make it back? Is this everything? If I really am the prince, the last descendant, then why the hell am I in foster care? The panic and conflicting thoughts inside me have become toxic and are about to explode into a rage.

Danielle's entire energy shifts. She puts her hand on my shoulder. "Johnny, are you okay?"

I take a deep breath and look up at her. My words come out a little too harsh. "So, what's taken you so long to say anything?"

Her eyes soften. She drops her hand and her attitude. "Well, I had to make sure before sounding like a complete idiot. You can't just walk up to a normal teenager and mention the spirit world. They would probably freak." A slow smile spreads across Danielle's face. "Sometimes I do wish I could show them what exactly is whispering in their ears." She leans toward me. "They're so scared of flesh-eating zombies. Imagine if we could show them the disfigured Troglodytes hiding under human flesh, walking our halls, and hunting unclaimed teenage souls. Now that would be apocalyptic!"

I laugh with her, although my mind is still racing. Five minutes ago, I thought I was the only one around here from Shamayim. Not only am I surrounded, but I'm supposedly the last descendant, the prince who will either save human souls or take them! I feel the need to run or destroy something. Hopefully, Danielle will drop the whole prince rescue plan.

No such luck. The moment we stop laughing, she looks at me and jumps back in right where she left off. "Johnny, we have to do something about this. Let's go underground and bring them back. I know where a portal to Dunabi is. I've watched a certain Trog go below ground transforming from a blond beauty to the most disgusting beast you can imagine." Danielle shivers and then stares into my eyes. "So the real question is, are you going to help me bring our parents home before it's too late?"

I stare at the ground. My dad's words drum through my mind. He made me promise. I look up at Danielle, "I can't."

She explodes, "Why not? If any of us can, it's you!"

A sudden coldness hits my core. Why don't girls ever think about anyone but themselves? She assumes because I'm the prince that I can just walk into the middle of the dark world and demand our parents' release. My fists tremble, I stand up. "I just can't!"

Not a word escapes Danielle's mouth, but I can feel her cringe as I turn my back and stomp away. I slow down and clear my throat. I should go back and try to make her understand. My shoulders drop. It's no use, she won't listen.

I stuff my hands in my pockets and walk up to the trampoline. Canyon hops off right in front of me and slugs me on the arm. "Hey, you wanna go play Black Ops?" I can feel Danielle's eyes burning holes all through me. I look over my shoulder, but Danielle is gone. Someone else is staring, but who? I look all around. No one's looking at me except for Canyon who's now tilting his head up.

"You don't have to commit to a long-term relationship. It's just a game or two. Do you wanna go or not?" His eyes roll back down at me.

I turn my head to Canyon. "No commitment, huh?"

He pushes me toward the house. "Come on, turd."

We walk in the back door to a dark room except for the light from the Dallas Cowboys playing football on the big screen. Danielle's words keep running through my mind. Who else is from Shamayim? I walk around the couch when suddenly a deep roar stops me dead in my tracks.

"No! You have got to be kidding me!"

A huge figure leaps out of the recliner in front of me. My black belt training takes over. In less than two seconds, I locate the point of danger and its line of attack. Then I jump to move myself out of harm's way, which causes me to bump into Canyon, knocking him into the wall. Step 3, strike. I don't hesitate and prepare to give it my best hopping sidekick.

At the exact same moment, Ray yells at the television. "Dallas Cowgirls strike again! Why can't Romo ever complete a pass!"

Canyon pushes me away from him. I take a few steps and drop my arms when I realize the attacker is just Ray. I look at Canyon and shrug my shoulders. It's not my fault, I didn't know a man that large could move that quickly. On the other hand, it makes complete sense.

He scowls at me, but yells at Ray, "Dad!"

"Huh?" Ray gives us a quick glance over his shoulder, but looks right back at the game as if his eyes will burn out of his sockets if removed from the TV for too long. Ray stutters, "Oh. Sorry."

The news guy breaks in on his game. Ray grunts and plops down into his recliner.

"Special Report with Matt Buchanan. The Bureau of Health has announced that over the last three weeks, there has been a 37 percent increase in the amount of coma cases across the country."

The screen shows a hospital wing full of patients. "Hospitals are running out of resources to care for the excessive number of patients. The Bureau is investigating the sudden increase with preliminary reports of a genetically modified organism to blame. The government assures us that the situation is under control. Tune in at ten o'clock for the full report." The screen flashes back to a commercial for dog treats.

Canyon grunts, "If they only knew."

I turn to look at Canyon, but catch Ray giving him a fatherly shut-up glare. He changes to a smile as soon as he sees me looking. I smile back and decide to interrogate Canyon later when there aren't any witnesses.

Canyon mumbles, "We're wasting valuable Black Ops time. Let's get out of here." He motions for me to follow him.

Ray doesn't even notice as we leave.

We get upstairs and Canyon starts setting up the Xbox.

"Canyon, can I ask you something?"

"You just did." He untangles the controllers and hands me one.

"Funny. So why'd you say that earlier about the people in a coma?"

"Let's just say people think they have everything figured out, but they don't." He selects a map for our game and sits back against the bed.

"I'm guessing you know more than the news guy, huh?"

He smirks. "I just know it isn't as simple as something we're eating." Black Ops starts, and Canyon's eyes are glued to the screen. He's officially a game zombie. Within five seconds, he lifts his controller in the air and yells, "That's bull, I shot him first!" as if I'm not even here.

I take a deep breath and try a little shock treatment. "Is that why the Guardians moved me here?"

Canyon drops his controller and turns to face me. "Who told you the Guardians sent you here?"

I cock one eyebrow. "You can stop pretending that everything is normal around here. It took me a little while to figure it out, but I know who you are."

He motions for me to shut up and crouches down to look out the door. No one's around so he closes it and moves in close. "We've been told this mission is top secret. How did you find out?"

"I'm the prince, Canyon. Shouldn't I know who my people are?"

"Good point." Canyon halfway shrugs.

My face gets hot. "You knew I didn't know!"

ONE PRINCE, TWO KINGDOMS

"We all know you don't know, but now you know and they're gonna blame me, but I didn't..." He stops ranting and drops his voice along with his eyebrows. "Who told?"

I tilt my head. "Is that really important?"

"Good point." Canyon halfway shrugs.

I lean forward. "How strict are the terms of protection?"

Canyon shifts and finally sits on his hands. "Strict enough that you are to be in line of sight at all times."

"At all times? How many Guardians are on duty?" I ask.

Canyon chuckles. "Basically all of them."

"Oh reeee-ally? So besides the Johnson clan, who else?" I ask.

Canyon starts shaking his head. "Uh-uh. I'm not saying another word." He closes his eyes and blows his cheeks out humming "Don't Worry, Be Happy."

I punch his leg. His pitch turns into a yelp. I smile and tilt my head. "I am the prince. Don't you think you should care more about my orders?"

His eyes bug out. "Have you met my dad!"

I laugh. "Very true, but I won't say a word."

Canyon rolls his eyes. "Fine, the main ones are my parents, Maestro, and Ms. Sara, but there are some more teachers and students. Oh, and the mailwoman plus the guy that works at the gas station."

"Well, hell, am I the only project going? What about the rest of the world?" I'm feeling a bit over-protected and suddenly claustrophobic. Over the last few years, my parents have been training *me* to protect the twelve. Never did I imagine that *I* was the final descendant that everyone would have to protect.

"You're a funny guy, now, aren't ya?" Canyon bugs his eyes out as if I'm a complete idiot. "If something happens to you, then we don't have a world, remember?"

If something happens to me? The reality of being the prince is starting to settle in my stomach. I take a deep breath and refocus. "Okay, so what's the deal with all the people in a coma?"

Canyon lowers his chin. "Their souls have been taken."

"By who?" I start popping my knuckles.

Canyon grits his teeth. "Troglodytes."

Memories that had been safely tucked away make a sudden reappearance. *There's an army of Trog-lodytes, the beasts of darkness, shifting and grunting as they descend a stonewall. One of the creatures crawls up behind my mom like a bobcat about to pounce on its prey. Horror flashes across my face. Mom mouths, "I love you" and nods as if she knows what's coming. I suck in a breath, but before I can scream, it grabs my mom's feet and slams her face first into the floor, dragging her away unconscious.*

I was there. I watched them take her soul, and I did nothing!

My voice jumps out of my throat, "Why?"

He looks at me as if wondering if I'm serious. "It's part of the whole battle for souls between Shamayim and Dunabi. Johnny, you seriously need to catch up. How are you going to be the prince if you don't know anything?"

That's exactly what I was just thinking. I've been raised in the light, learning to fight against the beasts who prey on the weak. Now they have my mom. It's time to face the dark. I stand up. "I need to go to Dunabi."

Canyon twists and stares with eyebrows at full attention. "Do you wanna get killed?"

"By who, the light or the dark?" I ask while pacing back and forth.

"Good point." Canyon halfway shrugs again.

I stop and look at him. "You say that a lot, you know?"

Canyon gives me a quick smirk. "I can tell this mission isn't going to be as easy as we had hoped."

I roll my eyes. "I try."

Canyon turns back to restart his game. "You know if you go I'm going with you, right?"

I cannot believe he thinks I need a babysitter. "It's okay, I'm a big boy. I haven't been afraid of the dark since I was a little kid."

Canyon shivers. "It's not what you can or cannot see that you should be afraid of."

I cross my arms. "You're not going to scare me out of going."

Canyon's voice rises. "Fine, just don't go without me." Then he mumbles, "I frickin' hate the dark." The game zombie is back.

I escape to a long, hot shower. By the time I get back to my bed, Canyon is snoring. Once my head falls onto the soft pillow, I'm asleep.

❦

"Johnny." I hear my mom's voice calling me. "Johnny."

I'm standing in a sterile white hallway in front of an open door. I see my mom lying in a hospital bed with her eyes shut and tubes all over her. She has an IV and a breathing tube connected to a ventilator that sustains her life.

I rush to her side and gently put my arms across her frail body. Tears stream down my face onto my mom's hospital gown.

"Johnny."

I sit up, expecting to see her awake and talking, but her eyes are still shut and the machines are still pumping. I look around, trying to understand why I can hear her calling me even though she's not awake.

I grab her hand and beg. "Mom, talk to me again. I'm here. It's me, Johnny. I'm here."

Something grabs my arm. Mom is sitting up in her bed with wide eyes. She lifts her free hand and points to the wall. I turn my head. A huge man in a dark suit is standing in front of the window. He raises his right hand casting the wall of dirt from behind him into the room like a tidal wave crashing on top of us. I block my eyes and try to cover my mom. I can feel her trembling as the dirt rains down.

Finally, it slows down enough to see the room's covered from ceiling to floor in dark brown soil. The machines, tubes, bed, and window are all gone. We're in an empty dirt room. My mom curls up in the corner and starts to rock. I put my arm around her and try to comfort her. All around us, the walls have been knocked down. Her room has opened up, facing an endless hallway of dirt caves. Each tiny room has a person curled up in the corner, rocking.

I turn to my mom. "Where are we?"

She puts her shaking finger to her mouth and whispers, "Dunabi."

I have to ask one more question. "Who are all these people?"

Her eyes dart toward the man and her entire body trembles. Her mouth appears to be frozen as she forces another whisper, "The Missing."

There are as many caves as grains of sand by the sea. I want to know more, but the man turns and glares at my mom as if she has committed a crime. He reaches into his suit jacket. I see the handle of a .22 revolver. I hold my breath. There's no time, I have to choose to cover my mom or attack this huge man. His hand is on the gun. My adrenaline spikes. I'm ready to attack.

Just as I let go of my mom, another wall of dirt blinds me. I hear scuffling. My eyes adjust, and I see a man in white pummeling the man in black. I back up to protect my mom. They roll on the floor, throwing punches, and grabbing for the gun. I look around the room. There's only one way in and one way out.

The man in white yells, "Johnny, get her out of here!"

I know that voice. I look down at the man's face, for a split second his eyes meet mine and I see his twitching eye. Dad? Words refuse to come out of my mouth.

"Johnny, now! Get your mom out of here!" he yells, as he takes an elbow to the jaw and loses his grip on the gun.

I ignore his orders and lunge toward the man in black. He reaches back to punch my dad, but I grab his arm in midair. With one swift jab, he slings me across the floor. I push up to my feet and prepare for attempt number two.

"Johnny, go!" Dad's voice begs. He never begs. I stop and stare at the two fighting. There's nothing I can do, I'm only making things worse.

My mind tries to process the fact that my missing dad is fighting a man with a gun and telling me to get out of here when suddenly, there's a deafening pow!

Blood pools below the two men on the floor.

❧

My eyes pop open. The dreams are back.

SHE NEEDS ME

CANYON ASKS ME, "Who you riding with?"

I look at Caylee and then at Danielle. "Who's gonna let me drive?"

Caylee shoots me down. "Not me!"

I turn to look at Danielle and flash my million-dollar smile. It has never failed me before. I watch Danielle's face tilt down as a half smile spreads. Score! She motions for me to take the driver's seat right in front of her. I run and hop on. Danielle scoots up right behind me and wraps her arms around my waist. My breath catches in my lungs.

Canyon smirks and spins his four-wheeler around, slinging rocks everywhere.

I follow him up a steep little hill, which opens up to a wide dirt path leading to a huge radio tower in the distance. Canyon disappears into the woods, jumping every pothole and rock he can find.

Caylee pulls up next to me. "You wanna race?"

"Uh, yes!" Danielle yells.

I laugh. "Where to?"

Caylee points ahead. "To the tower and back."

"Just say when." I rev the engine. Caylee leans over her handlebars and mocks me revving my four-wheeler. We exchange competitive glares and wait for the countdown.

Danielle squeezes my waist, "On your mark, get set, go!"

I yell, "Hold on!"

Danielle presses her body into mine. The four-wheeler skims over the rocks like a boat on water. Caylee is not far in front of us. We wrap around the tower and rush back. The finish line is approaching. Canyon's four-wheeler jumps out of the woods right in front of us. Caylee speeds around him, and I end up stuck in the back. We all slide to a stop.

Caylee immediately starts bragging, "I beat all of you!"

Danielle squeezes my waist. "We were just being nice."

Canyon laughs. "Yeah right, Danielle. Y'all really think you're fast, huh?"

Caylee clears her throat. "Who finished in first place?"

"Yeah, but you're no match for me!" As Canyon speaks, I feel the challenge heating up the air around us.

"Oh, yeah, how 'bout you put your money where your mouth is?" Caylee hurls that at Canyon like a firm punch in the gut.

"No problem, I need a few extra bucks. How 'bout ten?"

Danielle sneaks a quick insult into the conversation, "Ten what, cents?" She laughs a little too loud in my ear, but I don't mind.

"Ten it is. Girls versus boys, race to the tower and back." Caylee takes control.

Canyon refuses to follow her terms. "No. Let's take this off-road. Up the hill and back around."

Danielle states the obvious, "Guys, we're short one four-wheeler."

I smile. "Let's do this relay style. They have to jump off and we jump on." I twist and look behind me at Danielle, who smiles and nods.

Now that the race details are worked out, we all drive over to the fence that guards the tower. Canyon and Caylee line up. Danielle counts down and they take off through the rough trails. I sit on my four-wheeler with Danielle still sitting against me.

We hear Caylee yell at Canyon, "You're sooooo fast!" and then she bursts out laughing.

Canyon yells back, "Heck, yeah! Eat my dust!" Then we hear their engines jump up to the next gear.

Danielle's still behind me with her arms around my waist. "So you seem to be getting along well at school. No more tours needed?"

I chuckle. "No tours. It's better than I thought it would be." An awkward silence fills the air.

She drops her arms and hops off the four-wheeler. "How do you like the Johnsons?"

I take a moment to think of a cool response. "They're pretty cool." Wow, that was epic, Johnny.

Danielle nods her head. "They've helped me a lot."

"Have you heard anything about your parents?" I kick my legs over to one side to face her.

She's holding a small branch and fidgeting with the leaves. "Nope, have you?" She looks up and locks me in her icy blue eyes.

I shake my head and look down to hide my smile. "So, what's the plan to get our parents back?"

With a huge smile, I look back up. Danielle's eyes are bright and she's coming straight for me. "We go to Dunabi and get them."

"You make it sound so simple." I drop my smile, but keep my eyes on her.

Danielle's hands are flopping back and forth as she speaks faster than I knew was humanly possible. "It should be. The guards are near-sighted and extremely self-centered, which makes them pretty easy to get around."

My eyebrows relax. "Okay, but what about the Celestials and the possibility of being taken?"

Danielle's eyes lose their sparkle. "I figure we can deal with that as it happens. Dunabi's not all bad. That's like saying Texas is a horrible place because it has prisons in it."

I pause. "So you're not against the dark kingdom?"

"Johnny, we all have a dark side. What are you afraid of?" Her arms are folded, and she's looking straight into my eyes.

My muscles tense. "Not afraid, just cautious."

Her eyes narrow. "So are you in?"

I want to say yes, but instead I shrug my shoulders. Danielle's chin lowers to her chest.

I try to cheer her up. "That depends, when do you plan to go on your little rescue mission?"

She looks away. I want to know more, but Canyon and Caylee come racing around the corner through the large opening with Canyon yelling, "Cheater!"

He slides his four-wheeler around and hops off. I jump on and hit the gas riding off into the thick trail to begin our team's second and final lap to victory. Danielle isn't far behind me. I rush through a small clearing even though briars slap me on my bare legs. The instant I break through the thick brush and turn onto the larger path, I hear Danielle gasp and thud. Her engine goes silent.

Everything in me wants to win, but I cannot leave Danielle. Without a second thought, I turn around and go back, expecting to find a broken leg or blood gushing from her head. I rush over the small hill through the patch of briars and shut off the engine when I see her four-wheeler kissing a huge tree. "Danielle!" Oh my God, she's been thrown off. My face turns white. I peer into the trees, twisting around to look everywhere. "Danielle!" Something moves in the brush ahead of me. I start my four-wheeler and drive closer, expecting to find Danielle mangled and bleeding to death. I jump off and run through the brush, screaming her name, but she's nowhere to be found.

I feel eyes from the woods trained on me. I swear something moves in the trees beside me. I am freaked. I race back to my four-wheeler and speed down the path to get help. Tension is shaking every muscle in my body. Where could she be? The moment I see the twins, I start yelling, "Did Danielle come back this way?"

Caylee answers, "No, why?"

"I heard her crash. So I went back to find her and she's gone."

Canyon and Caylee exchange a look as if they know something I don't know. Canyon orders, "Take us where y'all were."

Caylee and Canyon hop on the back. I spin around and drive back up to the briars, "I was up there," I point over the hill, "as soon as I heard her crash, I turned around and rushed back to help her, but she's not here. I know she didn't have time to run off and her four-wheeler is still here." The twins hop off and search for blood. I look through the trees. "It's like she's completely disappeared into thin air!" When the words left my mouth, it's like they entered my brain for the first time. I understood what the twins' look meant. Danielle went after her parents, without me.

I turn to Canyon. "We have to follow her."

"No, we don't."

Caylee chimes in, "Johnny, you're not of age yet. It's too dangerous."

My blood's getting hot. I'm so tired of everyone telling me it's too dangerous! I laugh. "Dunabi could be my future throne! Maybe you're worried about *your* safety, not mine!"

Caylee doesn't hold back. "Are you kidding me? Do you really think we're so selfish that we won't risk our own safety for the kingdom? You wanna go, let's go, but let me warn you, there will be things that appear beautiful, but below ground are horrid and hungry. You might be their future prince, but until you take your throne, they'll do everything they can to remove you from existence."

My heart skips a beat. "Why would they kill me? What've I done?"

"It's not what you've done, it's what you *will* do. They don't want any power over them, and everyone knows: remove the twelve and the kingdoms will fall."

I sit back on my four-wheeler. "So they're trying to kill me?"

"Why else would you have the highest order of protection?" Canyon asks.

"Then I'm not safe anywhere." My stomach feels rock hard.

"Exactly!" Caylee throws her hand in the air.

I sit there in silence with my head down. Then what will it hurt to go to Dunabi? If they won't help me, I'll find my own way. I know better than to say whatever pops into my head, so I'll keep my mouth shut.

Within seconds, Susan and Ray are running up to us. They got here quick and on foot. Definitely warriors.

Susan looks at me. "Tell us every detail."

Dinner is not the same. Everyone knows Danielle ran away, and no one's willing to say a word. If only I had agreed to go with her, she wouldn't be underground. Alone.

I help clean up and drag myself through the living room to the stairs. Susan stops me at the base of the steps. Her presence calms me like pure baking soda on a grease fire.

"Johnny, I know you're upset, but I promise we're doing everything possible to find Danielle." She pauses. My emotions feel externally manipulated as she continues, "If something were to happen to you, for example if you ran away, it would complicate things. Then, we would have to change our focus to finding you. Do you understand what I'm saying?"

How did she know what I was thinking? I manage to say, "Yes, ma'am. I understand."

I don't think she believes me.

I'm so exhausted. Once I finally make it to my bed, I'm out.

⌘

I'm drowning in darkness. The hair on the back of my neck stands on end. I try to focus my eyes, but there's no way to see anything without light. I stand still, attempting to use my other senses to figure out where I am and what's going on here. A burning ash smell lingers in the still, warm air. Something rustles over to my left, followed by a mumble, as if someone's trying to speak with tape covering their mouth. I slowly raise my arms to see if I can feel anything around me. Nothing in front, nothing to my left or right, but close behind me is a cold, rough vertical surface. I turn slightly and follow the cold stone wall. Trying to be silent, I press on toward the only dim light up ahead.

Suddenly, something runs across the exposed flesh on my foot. I try to keep from freaking out and force myself to walk faster.

If only I could see.

As I progress closer to the light, groaning emanates from a man who's obviously in tremendous pain. Apprehension grasps my whole body. Do I really want to see what's in front of me or should I turn back? I try to look behind me, but it's pitch black. I proceed to the light.

Weakly, the light exposes the ground in front of me. I can now see the stone wall to my right. Spiders and rats speed by me, running into the darkness. This can't be good. I back up against the wall until they pass. The groaning is getting louder and more frequent.

New sounds fill the dark, musty air. Chains slap against stone and flesh followed by a deep, desperate scream. Even though fear squeezes me in its fist, I have to see. I come to the end of the wall and see shadows moving in the light. They belong to misshapen humans moving around like a pack of hyenas, hovering over a dead carcass. No wonder the rodents are escaping; they don't want to become one of those things.

One is extremely large with broad shoulders and a large head with tusk-like teeth protruding from his mouth. Another creature is a short, hairy humpback that's pacing very quickly from one place to another, as if looking for its next meal. Two others are in the back, but I can't make out what exactly they are. Let's just say I don't want to get any closer. All I know is that I'm somewhere I don't want to be, but it's too late, I'm here.

There's a wall across the room with someone chained to it. The poor man is disfigured from the obvious beatings he's endured. I want to get closer, but I know they'll see me.

One of the beasts grabs the man's face and demands, "Tell me where he is! You cannot hide the prince from the darkness forever! We are everywhere."

The man quietly responds, "Greater is he that is in me, than he that is in the world."

My heart's pierced by these words. I've heard that many times before. The man is no stranger, he's my dad!

Without thinking, I jump away from the wall and charge at the huge beast. With a primal yell, I demand, "Let him go!"

The four beasts charge at me.

The small one has my leg, the large one falls to the floor after I hit him, and the other two are coming at me when a white flash protects me from sure death. The beasts redirect their attack to the white being. I'm knocked to the floor. Looking up, my eyes meet my dad's eyes. He smiles at me and I lunge toward him. A beast diverts my attempt and hits me hard on my right ribcage. I fall against the floor in front of my dad and gasp for air.

Dad yells, "Johnny, get out of here!"

∽∾

I sit up and hit my head on the bunk above me. The clock's red glow blinks 2:22 a.m. My head's swimming. Did I really just find my dad? I want to run for help, but they're all sleeping. Instead, I lay back and hope my dreams will take me back.

∽∾

"Johnny." I hear my mom's sweet voice. "Sweetheart, it's going to be okay."

"Mom, where are you?"

"Johnny, you have to find me. Only you can."

I can see my mom's face. She's so dirty and bruised. Her hair is a mess and she looks weak. I can see the same stone wall behind her that my dad's chained to.

"Tell me how, Mom. What about Dad?"

"He's here with me, son." She weeps. "It's all my fault. I'm sorry, but you have to save us. Help us, Johnny. *You* are the only one who can."

Her voice fades. I beg her not to leave me. All I can hear is her saying sorry over and over followed by fading sobs. The image of my mom turns into darkness. I'm alone, again.

ᏇᏇᏇ

I gasp for air as my eyes pop wide open. I'm back in the bedroom with Canyon in the bunk above me. He thrusts his head over the bunk rail and hangs upside down to ask me, "You all right down there?"

"I think I'm sick."

He pulls himself up quickly and orders, "Oh no! Don't you puke in here! You go to the toilet, and I'll get Mom."

I chuckle. "Not gonna puke, Canyon."

"Okay, good. I hate puke." Canyon hops off the bed. "So what's wrong?"

I lift the blankets and my whole right side is already a deep blue. "Wow. How'd you do that?" he asks.

"I'm not sure. I know it sounds crazy, but I think it happened in my dream."

He doesn't look shocked, but prods me on with a dramatic nodding of his head while bugging out his eyes.

"Canyon, I've got to go to Dunabi, now."

"It looks like you've already been."

"Very funny. They've got my dad chained to a wall. They're threatening to kill him! And my mom is…" My voice cracks. I rub my face and take a deep breath.

"Let me get Mom and Dad." He turns to leave the room.

"No!" I try to jump up, but my side slows me down.

Someone knocks on the door. Canyon opens it and lets Caylee in.

She jumps right in the conversation as if she was here the whole time, "Johnny, you can't just go barging into Dunabi; that would be a suicide mission." At the same time, we look at each other with glassy eyes. I'm sure we're all thinking of Danielle.

"You can help me or not, either way I'm going." I brace myself on the bunk bed. "I'm the prince. I have authority over the heights of Shamayim and depths of Dunabi. I can't just sit here and ignore what's going on all around me." My ribs throb and force me to sit back down.

Canyon points at my side. "Just because you have the authority doesn't mean you are ready to use it."

I look up at him. "You're right, but doing what I should won't protect my family or keep Danielle from being killed." I stare back at him like a cornered animal. "Think of all the Missing! How long are we going to sit back and *think* 'How sad' when we can get off our butts and *do* something about it?"

Canyon turns to Caylee. They exchange a long look and then nod at the same time. She explains, "We'll take you on one condition."

"Okay, what?" I ask.

"You have to trust us," she replies.

I nod. "When do we go?"

Caylee explains, "At midnight."

"That's my—"

"We know," Caylee interrupts.

Canyon grins. "You will never forget this birthday."

My spine crumbles. "It will be too late by then."

Canyon replies, "Not exactly. Midnight is liminal: not here nor there. It's the perfect cover and *we* will have the element of surprise!" He nudges me with his elbow.

Great, I love being the surprise.

BUT I FUMBLE

AFTER A BUNCH of Tylenol and dressing at the speed of an eighty-year-old man, I force myself to go to school.

First period, athletics, the coaches aren't exactly supportive of a kid sitting out because mommy said so. I try to stay out of their way until the bell finally rings.

Second period, Mr. Brooks announces that the winning review team gets to leave class first. Shay's as beautiful and bossy as ever. After each question she whispers the answers loud enough for everyone to hear. It's no surprise when our team wins and races out of the class victoriously.

Shay catches up to me. "You didn't call."

I glance over at her. "Yeah, sorry, we had a lot happen last night."

"You talking about Danielle?" Her arms wrap around her books.

"Yeah." How does she know?

Shay puts her hand on my back. "Don't worry about her. She runs away all the time and shows back up sooner or later."

My neck stiffens. I look at her cold face and realize she's dead serious. We walk in silence to the end of the hall. All I can think about is Danielle. When I stop at my locker, Shay looks over her shoulder and winks at me as she disappears into our science class. Suddenly, my feet won't work right. I fumble inside and drop in my seat before the tardy bell.

I slump down and stare at Ms. London while she barks a lot of stuff at us. My eyes sway to the empty seat next to me. Heaviness presses down on my chest. I quickly turn my empty stare back to the front of the room.

Class is not the same without Danielle.

The bell rings and students are everywhere. Of course, the lock on my locker won't open, which slows me down even more. The tardy bell rings right when I slam the metal door shut. No sense in rushing now. I walk around the corner and see Canyon slipping out of his class.

He looks at me and uses some teenage sign language that I think means what-the-heck-are-you-doing-in-the-hall.

I motion back runnin-late-Einstein.

He catches up to me, laughing. "Three hallways and you're tardy? Really?"

"I have my reasons. What are you doing?"

Before he can answer, the wicked witch of the third hall, Mrs. Monk, steps in front of us with her ginormous chest threatening to poke one of our eyes out. "Show me your passes," she demands.

Canyon speaks up, "I'm running an errand for Mr. Frazier," he points to me, "and he's a new kid."

"I don't care if you were sent by the president and he's been here his whole life, where's your passes?" She grinds her teeth.

My muscles jump. I really don't like this lady. I look at Canyon hoping he will do something before she eats us. He looks like he's off in a distant daydream. Great. I turn to Mrs. Monk preparing to blabber about my locker getting stuck, but she's in a trance too. I look back at Canyon. He's not blinking. I look up and down the hallway hoping there aren't any witnesses as Canyon alters the witch's thoughts.

The short lady's body jolts as Canyon lets go of her mind. She growls back to life, "Well, you two better hustle and next time, bring a pass."

Canyon smiles as we walk past her and gives a sincere, "Yes, ma'am."

Mrs. Monk disappears into the first classroom on the left, giving us one second to make our escape before she changes her own mind. We speed walk to Maestro's door, the last one on the right. I knock on the door and drop my chin to give Canyon a shame-on-you glare.

Canyon shrugs his shoulders. "What? A little mind bending never hurt anyone." He laughs and walks away, vanishing around the corner.

Maestro's door opens. I sigh, and go inside.

The room is dark. Where's everybody? A sick feeling crawls up my spine. I want to run, but it's too late now. I'm standing in the center of Maestro's classroom trying to hide in the shadows. The pitter patters of feet move across the room. I twist, bumping into the table, and peer into the darkness. Nothing. I put my hand out and move around to the other side near the wall. The number of rustling feet doubles.

Something pulls my pant leg. I swat and hit a hairy thing that lets out a blood-curdling scream. I back up against the wall, darting my eyes through the darkness. What the heck is that? Whatever it is, it's short and makes a lot of noise. I climb on top of a shelf, hoping to be too high for the rodents to find. More feet scurry around the room, sounding like they are coming toward me! I pull my feet up to my body. My chest hurts.

I consider yelling for Canyon, but I don't want these things to hear me. Maybe they're just looking for something to eat. Oh, Gawd, why did I have to think that? I pull my feet up higher. Then I feel something scratch my neck. I jump and turn to meet a pair of deep orange eyes that belong to a foot-tall hairy creature standing on its hind legs. It slaps its claws against my cheek and runs off. My natural instincts take over. I jump off the shelf prepared to kill, but the sound of multiple feet changes my mind. I run and jump on top of the table in the center of the room, ready to fight.

One by one, these things jump up on the table and scratch at me with their needlelike claws. I practice my karate skills and deflect them off, left and right. There are so many and they're so fast, soon I'm kicking two or three at a time. One makes it up my leg and is dangling from my shirt, stabbing me in the side like a nurse stabbing a needle into me and pulling it out just so she can stab me again. I'm trying to hit it off, but another one sees my weakness and climbs up the other side. The pain is too much. I'm the giant about to fall at the hands of the tiny. I fall to one knee and keep swinging. A squeal from below the table hurts my ears. They know they're winning.

A dark fog overtakes the room. Creatures start flying and hitting the wall. Then I hear a familiar voice, "Prince, get up and fight." The Hollow Man is beside me. He grabs the two off my back and cracks their heads together, dropping them on the floor. I sweep kick four of them off the table.

"Use your strength," he commands.

I fumble. "My strength?"

His face tightens.

I take a firm stance, but step out too far and stumble off the side of the table. The Hollow Man grabs me before I hit the floor and places me in the middle. Once again, he rushes straight into my chest. Pain takes me to my knees. I cower under the sudden possession, but refuse to collapse. The creatures are all over, scratching and stabbing me.

I hear the Hollow Man inside my head, "Focus your anger."

I feel the rage these stupid nasty things have ignited inside of me. Blood droplets trickle down my side and back from the needle punctures. I push off of the table and throw my arms out, scattering creatures all over the room. I stand tall and clench my fists. *No more!*

The Hollow Man screams, "No holding back, let go!"

At that second, I blow out a gust of air and release my fists. For the first time, I let go of my pain, my fear, and my anger.

I let go…of everything.

A bright light flashes, consuming the entire room, followed by a sudden darkness that chases around me like a rushing wind. The creatures scream in fear.

"Make them bow," the Hollow Man tells me.

The wind increases as I peer at the creatures. Without a word, they kneel before me. One by one, their tiny, gross bodies transform into teenagers. I recognize the kid from my science class and a few of the cheerleaders. Soon the entire student body is kneeling before me in complete awe of my power. I can feel the Hollow Man's desire for more, my desire for more. Every muscle trembles like right before passing out. Then I feel the Hollow Man rush out of my chest. I grab my chest and gasp for air, but this time I find the strength to stay on my feet. I will not fall. I watch him unite with the wind spiraling around me. A rushing sound fills my ears and grows into an eruption of cheers from the crowd before me as if they're at our homecoming pep rally. I hold my arms up and feel the wind encircling me, listening to the praise all around me.

Something clicks followed by a constant light that fills the room, blinding my eyes. I blink three times. Then the door squeaks shut. Reality hits,

I'm standing beside my desk with my arms in the air. A gorgeous redheaded substitute is peering at me with her emerald green eyes from Maestro's desk. I drop my arms down to my sides and look around to see if anyone else is watching my crazy behavior. The classroom is full of students working silently on their vocabulary out of the textbook. I look to the back of the room to check underneath the table for the Hollow Man or creatures, but they're all gone, leaving me to look and feel completely insane.

The substitute clears her throat. "May I help you, Mr. Boggs?"

I slide back into my seat and pick up my pencil, "No, ma'am, I just needed to stretch."

THE SUBSTITUTE BEAST

I'M SITTING IN my desk on the front row by the curtain. The large round clock on the wall is not ticking. I turn to the class. Everyone is in extreme slow motion. The air is thick with a distinct blue hue. I'm in the spirit realm. My brow crumples. Someone has pulled me out of normal time, but who and why? I want to look around, but I force myself to sit perfectly still, using my peripheral vision to watch everyone else move at a fraction of my speed. Not easy.

I try to switch time back, but someone is blocking me. Maybe the twins are playing a joke. I have forty-five minutes before the class's blink is over. I'm sure no one will notice if I get up and look around. I slip out of my desk and look at the back of the room. Nothing. I turn back to the front.

I'll bet they're hiding on stage. I take a few steps toward the curtain. Something moves behind me. I stop and turn my head to the left. The teacher's desk is empty. Fear swarms my body with heat. Where's the substitute?

A cold rush of air goes down my back. Before I can react, I hear a sexy whisper, "I knew you were the one."

I'm glued to the floor.

She walks around me, dragging her finger along my collarbone. "Who knew our future prince would be so powerful and oh so handsome." She stops in front of me and leans in, speaking with an alluring Southern drawl, "What will you ever do with little ole me?" She smiles. "I bet you can think of a thing or two." She closes the tiny space between us and kisses my neck. As if my body's made of metal, I'm sucked into her magnetic field of complete attraction. The gorgeous redhead wraps her arms around me and pulls me against her body, kissing her way to my lips. Blood pumps through my entire body. Something pricks my neck. I jump. My senses flood back.

What am I doing? My back stiffens. I push her back. "Who are you?"

"Does it matter?" she presses back toward me, but I back away.

"Yes, it matters. Your prince demands to know."

"Oooh, such authority." She laughs and walks around me. "Your Guardians are not very good at their job. Here you are and here I am, but where are they?" Her eyes sharpen as her voice deepens, "They're too late. Nothing can help you now."

I know I have to move, but where? How? As soon as my brain processes the choices, I dart to my right and slip behind the heavy velvet curtain. It's so dark that I have to feel my way around the props and other obstacles. I move as swiftly as I can without knocking anything over.

Within seconds, I hear the sinister voice laughing over my shoulder. I feel her breath on my cheek. It smells of burning ash, but feels like ice. "Do you really think you can outrun me, Prince?" she taunts.

I don't stop moving. She pushes my back against the stage wall and puts her finger in my chest. "The others are so afraid of you, the last Descendant," she says as she laughs, but she quickly turns dark and growls, "but I find you pathetic."

I continue moving along the wall, feeling for Maestro's office door.

"Tracking you was the easy part. Taking you will be the fun part," she grunts.

My hand skims across the stage walls. I feel the light switch, which I know is right next to Maestro's office. I'm close.

"You are weaker than I expected. Your training has been insufficient. Pity, you could have been great like your ancestors."

I stumble and knock over a Rubbermaid box full of wigs. While trying to avoid falling, I reach for the wall and find the doorknob! Quickly, I push the door open and slide into the office, slamming the door shut and locking it. The table next to the bookshelf slides right against the door, leaving room for me to crawl under the desk. My thoughts are racing: Think, Johnny, think! I need to find help. So much for line of sight protection. Then I hear laughter from behind the door.

"You are very intriguing, Prince Johnathan. Do you really believe hiding behind a door will stop my powers?"

Time to get out of here. I summon a portal and transport through the light into the living room at the Johnsons' house. I'm alone. Regret comes with the realization that everyone's either at work or at school. To my horror, the substitute is already standing in front of me, still laughing.

"Interesting choice of location, Prince. Were you expecting help? Where are your Guardians? Hmmm, they are not here, either. Maybe they should have enlightened you that citizens of Darkness could follow the light current of a transport into the kingdom of Light. You opened the way for me, Prince. Thank you."

I'm so confused. The Johnson home is protected from infiltration of any citizen of Darkness. This is supposed to be a safe place. I didn't open anything! There's no time to second guess why and where. I have to get out of here! Without hesitation, I decide where to go and make my move. Instantly, I'm looking at Susan sitting at her desk, frozen. Great, she's still in carnal time and space. I need her help, but I don't know how to transfer her into the spiritual realm. I start explaining everything to Susan, hoping she can hear me.

I put my hands on her desk and let the words flow, "Susan, I thought it was the twins, but she tricked me. Next thing I know, she has me pinned in Maestro's office, so I transported to your house. Then the crazy substitute pops up in front of me saying I let her in. I know she will be here any second, but I just needed to tell you so maybe you could help protect me." Then it happens. The substitute is standing in front of me, growing agitated. I have to tell Susan one more thing. So I whisper, "By the way, she's not very nice and doesn't smell right."

"Games are over, Prince." She approaches me and continues, "I have pursued you long enough. It is time for you to come with me." She stares into my eyes, spreading a cold numbness from my head all the way down to my toes.

This is hopeless. I cannot fight her, much less the others who have my parents. I want this to end, now. From the deepest parts of my soul, I can feel the hopelessness overpowering every ounce of resistance left inside of me. The substitute continues to glare into my eyes without blinking, taking every inch of my body captive. I'm no longer in control. A dark fog approaches with sounds of rushing water and flames licking the oxygen away. Everything in the world around me fades, until a firm voice comes from behind her.

"You are out of your territory, Iska."

HAS NO POWER

THE SUBSTITUTE TURNS away from me to look behind her. Susan is standing in front of her desk in celestial form looking like she's ready to open a can of whoopass. As soon as the substitute's glare leaves my eyes, I slump to the floor. My whole body is weak, and my head's pounding.

"Susan, we meet again," the substitute sneers.

"What's a demon doing in a high school classroom? Don't you deserve a better assignment than that?" Susan steps toward the beautiful redhead. I cannot believe this is the same Susan I live with. She's complete muscle behind her navy blue warrior dress uniform.

"Yes, yes, but it seems I am the only one capable of bringing the prince to Dunabi." The substitute side steps away from Susan.

"You forgot one thing. You have no power here," Susan smirks.

"What does this have to do with you? I'm here for the boy, not you!" The substitute bumps into a table, knocking a stack of books over.

"This is Hura territory. You must submit to my authority under King Sai. Trespassing breaks the treaty," Susan speaks firmly, as if in court, and continues to corral the substitute.

"I came under the prince's authority. He is a direct descendant of Queen Nara. Therefore I have the right to be here!" she screams as she points at me. Her back is now against the wall.

"Under the prince? You're saying he invited you here?" Susan squares up in front of her and interrogates.

The substitute squirms and manages to reply, "It was not an invitation per se, but I could not have followed unless he allowed me to."

"Unless you followed his teleport pathway by wring compression, which you know is against the treaty," Susan rebuts. "You have acknowledged breaking the treaty by your mere presence here. Now a second offence of forced wring compression will be added to your alleged war crimes. You are to be taken to the abyss to await your trial before King Sai."

The substitute drops to the floor, writhing in torment. She mutters a chant in an unknown language as if crying for rescue from her queen. A silver cord appears from nowhere and twists around her wrists, binding her hands together in front of her. The substitute's beautiful body changes before my eyes into a large, disgusting beast. Her gorgeous human features melt away as big, muscular, inhuman arms and legs break through, covered in red, coarse hair. Her head is huge with four horns curling up. Her dress is now a tight fitting shirt that barely covers her core. That thing kissed me! Ugh!

I feel something warm behind me. Before I can turn, I hear a deep, "Hey, Johnny. Looks like you have some explaining to do."

It's Ray. He walks past me. I cannot believe my eyes. In human form he's huge; now, in his spiritual form he's huger than huge. My jaw hangs open at his amazing appearance. He's so muscular and probably over nine feet tall. He has hair!

Susan must have read my mind again because she says to Ray, "I guess we do look a little different in our Celestial form." She looks back at me, smiling and straightening her navy blue jacket. "Do you approve, Johnny?"

"Uh, heck yeah! He's a beast," I belt out.

"You know it!" Ray brags with a wink and flexes his upper body like a proud body builder. Susan rolls her eyes.

Ray pats her on the arm. "You look beautiful too, babe." He kisses her on the cheek. Then he nods his head toward the substitute. "Well, I better get the other beast outta here." With a stern look, he says to me, "And. Johnny," my body cringes, "we will talk more about all of this tonight." He grabs the back of the sub's arm. "Off to the abyss we go, little lady." As soon as the words leave his mouth, he and the substitute beast are gone.

Susan immediately asks me, "How long have you been in the spiritual world, Johnny?"

"About forty minutes."

"Then we must move quickly, we have only five minutes left in the spiritual realm before your class's blink is over in carnal time. Let's teleport to the stage in Maestro's class so that we will remain unseen. Come now," she orders.

"Wait, I have questions!" I plant my feet, refusing to move.

"Your questions will have to wait until after school. We don't have enough time before your friends' blink is over. I'm pretty sure they will notice if you're gone and then suddenly flash back into your seat," she replies.

"No, wait a second! Why did she or it say everyone else was afraid of me?" I ask.

Susan can see I'm not about to give up. She hesitates and then responds with a sharp tone, "Because you are the last descendent, and with that comes powers above all the demons and even Celestials. And 'it' came from Dunabi, the queen's demon from the queen's domain. No more time, let's go."

"Wait, what portal did she use to get here from Dunabi?"

Susan tilts her head to the ceiling and sighs. "Portals are all around you and growing in numbers every day. Times are dangerous in the spirit world. We're trying to protect your identity and location, but the war is growing in intensity. Right now I need to get you out of the spiritual realm. I'll explain more later, Johnny, we must get you back."

"What's to stop them from going after my mom?"

Susan pauses and then answers in a monotone voice, "The Guardians are going to check on her now. Let's go." She disappears.

How does she expect me to go back to class and act as if everything is normal? I'm going to check on my mom myself. Just as I'm about to teleport to the hospital, something grabs my arm, and instantly, I'm on the stage beside Susan.

"What just happened?" I ask Susan.

"Well, I can't really let you run off into danger. I told you they're checking on your mom. Johnny, you've got to start trusting me. Let's get you back to your seat," she orders.

After all that I've been through, I'll never trust anyone, even a Guardian. For now, I'll listen, but after tonight, it's a different story. I return to my desk and act like I'm finishing my paper. In less than two seconds, time switches out of the spirit and back to the restrictions of carnal time.

Everyone's moving, sniffing, and whispering again. The classroom door opens, and I see Susan walk in with the principal. The substitute is gone, and they're discussing the situation. Of course there's no mention of beasts trying to kidnap me, just a mystery of the vanishing substitute. Susan watches our class until the principal gets one of the teacher's aides, Mrs. Monk, from another class to come fill in for Maestro.

Before Susan leaves, she walks over to my desk and points to my paper to give the appearance of instruction. I look up at her and she says, "Your mom's fine. Don't make any rash moves. There is always a consequence." She nods her head and leaves with a smile. I stare as she walks out of the door feeling like I should run, but forcing myself to stay in my seat.

The class around me is completely silent, but every time a pen taps or paper rattles, I have to look over my shoulder to check for lurking beasts. Mrs. Monk is eyeballing me. Everyone is completely deluded. If they knew what I knew, the alien apocalypse would feel like a normal day. The bell rings. I gladly rush out of there.

The rest of the day drags, finally ending with math. As I walk by, Danielle's empty chair screams out my name. My heart feels like it will explode. I grab my homework and sprint to Susan's classroom. When I get there, the room's empty and the lights are off.

Mrs. Monk stands at the door and asks, "Do you need something, Boggs?"

I START TO RUN

I STAND THERE and consider my options. One, punch Ms. Monk in the face. Two, tell her off. Or three, politely walk away.

I push myself to say, "No thanks," and walk away to find Canyon or Caylee.

The halls are stuffed full of kids, but none of them are the Johnsons. My adrenaline spikes. I go to the main hall and stand there, watching until it's a ghost town. The only choice left is the office.

I walk in and ask Mrs. Martinez, "Do you know where Mrs. Johnson is?"

"Oh, honey, she had to leave suddenly, and you were supposed to ride the bus. Let me see if I can catch your bus driver before he leaves the intermediate school," she replies and then fumbles through her rolodex. She dials a number and smiles at me.

When someone answers, she turns away from me and talks quietly, "I have a student who needs a ride, where are you? Okay, I can bring him over. It'll take just a second. Okay, bye." She grabs her purse and turns back to me, "Let's go, Johnny. They're going to hold the bus for you at the intermediate school. I'll drive you over there. It's only a mile down the road." I follow Mrs. Martinez out to her car. My stomach aches, telling me not to go, but I go anyway. She drives me to the back of the intermediate school and I board bus number 66. The bus driver is a big man with a huge cowboy hat.

He smiles with a yellow-toothed, tobacco-speckled grin and says with a thick country accent, "Take a seat, boy. We've been waitin' for you long enough."

There are a lot of kids who I don't know on the bus, so I sit all by myself next to a window. The ride's bumpy and long. With each mile, the bus drives closer to a thick patch of fog. I look at my watch, and it's 5:22 p.m. I've been on this bus for over an hour and there's still twenty kids or more left wanting to get off this hunk of junk.

As we continue driving into the fog, my gut aches even more. Something's wrong. With each stop to let a kid off, I think about running, but then I see the bus driver staring at me in his large rearview mirror hoping I will make the wrong move. I sit up tall and stare out my window.

A black SUV passes the bus. I look through their windows and count three figures. Then I see a pale face with dark eyes staring back at me. I grip the seat in front of me and watch the SUV jerk over into our lane and slam on their brakes. The bus driver doesn't even flinch. He brakes and pulls over behind them. I pop my knuckles and try to look for an escape through an alley or something, but the fog is so thick, all I can see is red taillights.

The bus driver looks at me. "This is your exit, boy." I don't recognize anything around me, but for some reason I know better than to argue. I slowly head for the bus door. My stomach hurts, but I push myself out of the bus before Cowboy decides to take me home for a snack. As soon as my feet touch the ground, the bus drives away.

"Prince, your chariot awaits."

Laughter fills the foggy air. I jump and turn to see two guys behind me, one on each side. "Let's go, Your Highness," the larger one commands as they push me toward the SUV.

I try to transport to the Johnson's house, but nothing happens.

My mind is racing. Maybe if I think as loud as I can, Susan and Ray will hear me. Over and over, I think about where I am and who has me, hoping someone can hear me.

Faintly, I hear, *Hold on, we're almost there. Don't get into that car!*

The two men are much bigger than me and we're approaching the door. How long do I need to hold on? I'm about to be forced into the SUV. I have to at least try to get away.

One guy lets go of my arm to open the car door. Like a flash, I use the side of the SUV to kick off as hard as I can while I push the guy still holding onto me. He stumbles forward, knocking his partner off balance and halfway into the car. He lets go of my arm and struggles to catch himself, but not before the door slams shut on his partner's arm.

They both yell, one from shock and one from pain. I take advantage of the chaos and sprint into the cover of the fog. I can't see a thing, but I hear an internal voice say, *Run to your right. There will be a fence, jump over it.*

I run to the right and jump a fence. A deep, angry bark keeps my feet moving. The voice commands, *Stop.* Against my better judgment, I stop. Then I see what the nearby dog is barking at, a human covered in scales curled up like a snake and looking right at me, ready to strike.

I look all around for somewhere to hide or run, but the human snake changes my mind. "You cannot outrun me, boy. It's over and you must go with me now."

Without thinking, I run for the fence. The man puts his hands on the ground and propels his body straight for me. His body slams into mine, knocking me to the ground.

He grabs me with his muscular arms and pulls my face close to his. "You think you are so strong, but you are not. I can take you down with one hand tied behind my back."

He releases me with one hand and pulls his legs underneath him. There has to be a way out of this. I twist, trying to get out of his grip.

His hand tightens and he laughs. "You're so weak."

I clench my fists and literally feel energy leaving my body through my eyes. You will never take me! Not without a fight. Then a flash of lightning hits him right in the chest. He falls to the ground thrashing in pain. The dog charges and attacks the man. I don't waste any time; I run.

Someone flips on the back porch light to the little house. I stop and crouch down to hide behind a big green bush. They open the back door, but I can't see who it is.

A sweet elderly voice floats from the house, "Is someone out there?"

I start to ask her for help, but the voice inside commands, *Don't move!*

I freeze. Each breath feels like I'm jumping up and down in the stillness all around me.

"Missy Moo, come on, girl. It's time to come inside," the elderly voice calls out to the dog. I think it might be a while before that dog is going anywhere.

A cloud of fog moves out of my way, allowing me to see the little old lady standing at her back door. She peers in my direction for what feels like an hour before she steps out far enough on her porch for me to get a good look. Out from under her robe swings a tail that curls up under the back of her robe and disappears. My back muscles twitch. So glad she's not my grandma. She mumbles something about a dead dog and goes back inside. The door shuts and locks. The lights go out one by one, and she's gone.

I let out a sigh and move slowly along the fence, searching for a gate. Every few feet, I look back at the house to make sure grandma is still asleep. Finally. I find the latch to the gate and slip out to the street in front of the house. Unsure of where to go, I hide in the shadows, moving to the main road. Hopefully the voice in my head will speak up anytime now.

The street is silent, the voice is silent, and I'm exhausted. Then I hear something to my right. Fearing the men from the SUV, I slide behind the nearest tree and look for who or what is coming my way. Three bodies push each other around, laughing. I press against the tree and try not to breathe.

INTO A NEW REALITY

THEY'RE ALMOST IN front of me when I recognize the short one. It's the crazy kid from school, Levi. He's with his two partners in crime, Steven and Aaron. I let out my breath and step away from the tree. They see me and start hollering my name.

In a goo-goo voice, Levi says, "Come here, Johnny," acting like I'm a little baby learning to crawl.

Steven asks me, "What are you doing out here alone?"

I answer, "Just trying to get home."

"I didn't know you lived over here," states Steven.

"I don't," I answer.

Aaron asks, "Then what are you doing here?"

"The bus dropped me off at the wrong stop." I roll my eyes.

"Shut the front door! I knew those bus drivers were crackheads." We all laugh at Levi. He tries to ignore our harassment and asks me, "So, what are you gonna do?"

I shrug my shoulders. "Guess I should call the Johnsons and tell them where I'm at."

Aaron slaps me on the shoulder, "Naw, man, it's early. At least have some fun before running back home."

Steven shoots an angry glare at Aaron.

Levi laughs at me. "Dude, you have got to live a little. YOLO!"

A smile creeps across my face. "Where's all this fun at?"

Levi raises his hands. "At the party of the year!" Then he hits Aaron and laughs some more. Levi acts like the Energizer Bunny on happy gas.

Aaron pipes in, "Yeah, you could say that."

Steven lowers his brow at Levi. "This party does not have an open invitation list."

Levi pats Steven's shoulder. "Relax man, Johnny's my plus one."

Steven rolls his eyes. "You and your BS are gonna ruin it for everybody."

Levi whispers to me, "Don't worry, bro. He's stressin' over a girl." He pumps his eyebrows and smiles at Steven. "A hot girl."

Aaron pipes in, "Are we gonna stand here and bicker like old women or hit the road?"

Levi puts his hand on his hip, "Yeah, Stevie. You wanna go?" Levi pushes Steven's shoulder and moves into a fighting stance, hopping side to side on his toes.

Steven hits Levi's hands. "No more acting like a frickin' idiot, you feel me?"

"Is a normal idiot okay?" Levi asks.

Steven stops in front of us and holds out his arm, forcing all of us to stop. His eyebrows drop and he growls, "Just shut your frickin' face or get the hell outta here."

Levi acts like he is zipping his lips, but this only irritates Steven.

Steven huffs and stomps off.

I crumple my eyebrows. Maybe I should call it a night. I'm not in the mood for anymore throw downs.

Levi must have read my mind because he smiles at me as if to say, "Don't leave me now," and motions the all-aboard signal.

They say curiosity kills the cat. Good thing they have nine lives.

I nod and follow them to the corner. We don't get too much farther before I hear music thumping. Steven turns and walks down another street. Then I see a million cars leading us straight to a huge house with lights flashing in the backyard and people everywhere.

Levi jabs Aaron.

Aaron jumps and yells, "Dude! Hands off!"

Levi laughs, but Steven turns around and yells in a whisper, "Yo, pump your brakes!"

Levi drops and shakes his head.

Aaron whispers, "Sorry."

I watch Steven cut across a flowerbed and crouch down beside a large brick home like a thief on his first job. He motions for us to lean in and whispers, "The gate is right there. I'll go in first. Wait at least ten seconds before coming in behind me." He stands, but stops to say one more thing, "Oh, and watch out for the neighbor's dog." He creeps off and slips through the open gate. Aaron goes next. Ten more seconds pass and I stand up.

Behind me I hear Levi, "Jooooohhhhhnnny," followed by a low growl. Sounds like Levi found the neighbor's dog. I look over my shoulder. Levi's face is pale. He points to his right. Expecting to see a huge mutt drooling on Levi's arm, I look over and see a vicious Chihuahua.

I try to scare the dog away, but the little rat just stares at me and cocks his head to one side. Well, that didn't work. He charges toward us, barking and showing teeth. I really don't want to get rabies from a six-inch wannabe rottweiler.

Only one thing to do, I yell, "Run!"

Levi hauls butt and flies through the gate. I slide in right behind him as Levi slams the gate shut at the perfect second. The little rat runs into the panels and claws at the wooden slats trying to get to us.

Levi's hands are on his knees as he pants for air. "Dude, I thought I was dead."

I cough. "You almost were."

He looks up at me and we both burst out laughing.

The loud music overpowers our laughter as if someone's trying to remind us why we're here. Levi lifts his chin and dusts off his T-shirt like he's heading in to a red carpet affair. He turns on a dime and saunters off toward the house. I force myself to swallow the laughter filling my mouth and walk silently behind Levi up the landscaped path to the back patio. My stomach drops. Two men are escorting Steven and Aaron through the house and out the front door.

Levi whispers, "This is our chance. Let's go before the bouncers get back."

We punch knuckles and head into the house.

First step in the door, we run into a pool table surrounded by people watching the game. To the right is a bar covered in red Solo cups. Levi darts for the beverages. I hang back and look around.

As soon as Levi picks up a drink, a lady walks up. "Hi, whose friend are you?"

Levi looks over his shoulder as if begging for help. I don't know anyone here. At least I didn't until I hear a high scream from across the room, "Johnny!" I look and see Shay running to me. She asks, "What are you doing here?"

"Uh, I, uh, we came to celebrate."

"That's cool. How do you know Chase?"

Levi smiles and nods. He now has a name.

I stammer, "Well, we actually just met a little while back."

"Really?"

"Yeah." I nod and try to act cool. Then I see two men walk up to Levi and grab both elbows. He shrugs and gives me thumbs up as they shove him out the front door.

Shay whispers, "There is no Chase. I saw you come in through the yard. What are you doing?"

A nervous laugh slips out. "If I told you, you wouldn't believe me."

She smiles. "Probably not, but since you're here, let's have some fun." I feel her arm wrap inside of mine and pull me away from the wall. She walks by the bar and hands me a drink. I look inside the cup and smell it.

"Chill, it's just a little fun in a cup." She laughs and pushes it to my mouth. I take a sip.

Hawaiian punch.

I ask, "So what exactly are we celebrating?"

She looks at me like I'm teasing her. "Leap year, what else?" Shay winks and pulls me into the next room full of people, beautiful people.

She drags me up to a group of girls. "Johnny, this is Maggie, Veronica, Celeste, and Hannah." I recognize Shay's clan from school. They're the locker Nazis. Danielle would hate this party. I imagine her standing next to me laughing in a high pitch, mocking every fake girl that walks by. A small chuckle rattles my chest.

Celeste puts her hand on my shoulder and leans in as if she's going to bite my neck. "You smell good. What is it?"

"Fierce," I reply.

"Mmmmm, so true." She stays close, smelling my neck.

Hannah feels my arms. "You know the type of cologne a man wears says a lot about him. Are you fierce, Johnny?"

My head is swimming. My senses are yearning for more. I feel their soft touch gliding up and down my arms and chest. Words are hard to form, "Y—yes, but only when needed."

Shay is standing across from me, smiling. Not a happy smile, but an amused smile. My lungs are speeding up. I need air.

"Excuse me, ladies. I'll be right back." I walk off to find a restroom. Shay doesn't move, but watches every step I take. There's a group of seniors from our school laughing and drinking the punch. Behind them is a door, which I'm sure is the restroom. I nod and go in like I own the place.

It's not the bathroom.

The room is dim, but I can see exactly what is happening. The energy and excitement pulls me in. I walk up to the central table and stand behind a beautiful woman in a red dress. She smiles and steps back, allowing me to get closer. Three men and two women are half dressed with their hands full of cards. The dealer is wearing a small amount of white lace that hugs her curves. I look down at the glass table and see the poker design on the green background is moving. Under the glass, two women are lying beside each other completely nude, but painted to look like a poker table complete with cup holders and stacks of poker chips in just the right places. I look up at the dealer. Her lace clothes are painted on too!

My collar suddenly feels tight. I look around the room to see each waitress has been painted to look like different characters from the famous "Dogs Playing Poker" painting. In the corner, a couple of men are examining the Border Collie's paint job. The Bulldog is bent over grabbing more drinks from behind the counter.

Now this is what I'm talkin''bout!

One of the waitresses walks up to me and offers a new drink. I'm in a trance, staring at the paint. She takes my cup and hands me a glass.

Without thinking, I take a drink.

My throat rejects the burning liquid. My coughing reflex makes it impossible to catch my breath. I find my way out the door, searching for the bathroom…again.

The lights in the hallway are down low and the music is pounding in my ears. I turn and follow the wall until I feel another door. This time, I look inside to confirm it's got a toilet. My head falls back. Thank God! I slip out of the hallway and put my cup down on the sink's edge. It falls over and spills the red liquid down the drain. I turn on the faucet and splash water all over my face while trying to put out the fire in my throat. Why didn't you use the glass, genius?

Finally, the coughing stops. I check my face in the mirror and make sure my hair is going the right direction.

Something taps on the window.

Curiosity pushes me to look. With each step, the tapping increases to a knocking sound. I pull back the curtain and see absolutely nothing. The wind is blowing, but there aren't any bushes or trees near the window. All is dark. I tilt my head and release the curtain. I turn my back and walk away.

Something pounds on the window.

I stop midstride, my body feeling heavy.

The pounding is loud.

Maybe it's Levi. I twist and open the curtain, smiling. Male and female, young and old shadowy faces fill every glass pane, laughing and crying then laughing again. My smile drops. They are scratching and pounding at the glass, trying to get out and begging me to help free them. I let go of the curtain and shuffle back against the sink.

The pounding continues.

My skin crawls over my muscles. I gotta get outta here! I twist away from the sink and stumble over my own feet, bracing myself with my back on the door. My eyes are locked on the window as I back out of the room, slam the door, and hold it shut as if the faces are going to come after me.

Something brushes against my back. I jerk my head to see two of the girls from earlier. I let go of the door knob and turn around, trying to act cool. They lean into my face and almost kiss my neck. Basically, they're all over me. This, I can handle.

Celeste whispers, "Have you ever been to heaven?" They both giggle.

I nod. "I sure have. What about you?" I keep looking at the bathroom door.

Hannah grabs my cheeks. "More than once, doll."

They laugh with hungry desire. Her fingers press into my cheeks a little too hard, but I don't mind.

Celeste asks, "Do you go alone?" She plays with my hair and breathes into my ear getting so close, but not making contact.

I cock my head sideways.

Hannah answers my unspoken question, "Or do you like it with one or two angels?"

I don't think we're talking about the same heaven. Desire swells inside of me. Maybe I do want to go to *their* heaven. Celeste's lips finally make contact with my neck. My eyes close. A warm heat goes down the back of my shirt. Her hand grabs my neck. I feel her fingers tighten. Her breath burns my cheek.

Then I hear, "Celeste!"

I jump to attention and open my eyes to see Shay with her hands on her hips. I look at the back of each girl's head watching the texture of their hair transform from dark and coarse to shiny and flowing. I stare at Celeste, blinking my eyes to clear up any tricks the drink might be playing on me. Then Celeste cuts her eyes at me as if she can feel my gaze. Holy crap! I hold my breath. Her eyes are no longer white with color. They are a deep blood red. I swear her teeth shrink and her eyes lighten up right in front of me.

Both girls back away from me as Shay walks up and slides under my arm with a smile. "It appears I found you at the perfect time." Shay glares at the girls and they back away, hissing.

My heart is doing backflips. "I guess you did."

Shay leads me out of the hallway and into a room full of strobe lights. The music pounds against my chest. Involuntarily, my head nods along with the bass. We're surrounded by oblivious people from school dancing and making out with one or two others. Every now and then, someone yells my name and gives me thumbs up or a fist bump. I'm living on full throttle desire, laughing and dancing, without a care in the world. My body feeds off of the energy around me.

Shay pulls me to the middle of the room. Her eyes stay on mine as she dances around me, moving up and down, swaying and spinning within an inch of my body. I forget all about the creepy girls and focus completely on the hot blond right in front of me.

The music slows. My heart follows the rhythm. Shay stops and stands toe-to-toe, staring at me with wide doe eyes. I take her hands and place them around my neck, dragging my fingers lightly down her arms until my hands find her waist. We are moving in complete sync with each other as her head falls to my chest.

I *feel* her slender, perfect body against mine and smell her sweet perfume, like cotton candy. Everything is perfect. Shay looks up into my eyes. My heart speeds up. Now or never. I lean down until our lips meet and eyes close.

Suddenly, her breathing stops. I pull back and look down to see if she's okay. She smiles. Everyone around us is still laughing and dancing. Shay grabs my face and pulls me back into her world. Our lips reconnect as the music continues to pound against my chest, but my ears only hear Shay's subtle breaths. Every second is in slow motion, intensifying every touch, smell, and sound from Shay. She pushes harder against my lips. I pull her in without hesitation.

A large hand slams onto my shoulder blade. My eyes snap open and my fists are clenched, ready to make some idiot pay for the interruption. Two guys are on each side of us. The hand on my shoulder belongs to a black-headed dude with pale skin. I recognize this guy. He sits across the room from me in history class. From a distance, he seems pretty cool, but today, someone needs a Snicker's bar.

"Back off, prick." He orders, but I'm not about to follow.

I push his hand off of my shoulder. A couple of girls gasp nearby. Well, he must be something special. I brush my sleeve off and glare. "I think you made a mistake, and I'm feeling generous. I'll let you walk, this time." I turn my back and take Shay back into my arms. Her body is stiff, but she forces a smile.

Angry laughter pushes against my eardrums. I look at Shay and hold up my finger. "One sec, babe." I turn around and swing.

He catches my fist. "Is that all you've got?" He laughs way too loud.

Plan B, I use my feet to sweep, but he doesn't budge. In fact, he's amused.

He looks at Shay. "What did you bring, a snack?"

He turns his head slowly, but his face is not the same. I know he was human five seconds ago. His teeth are unnaturally large and his eyes are red. He cocks his head to the right. "I told you to back off.

Now be a good little boy and step away before you get hurt."

The room feels extremely large, especially since everyone is hugging the walls. I clear my mind and stare. Before I can focus my energy, a force slams into my chest, hurling me across the room, smacking my head against the wall. I hit the floor. His laughter is like hot coals igniting the rage within. My muscles tighten. I stand and brush off like it was no big deal, although anger swells within me. With my head down, I tilt my eyes up just enough to focus my glare, sending my fury in waves straight for him.

I let go.

He grabs his chest and curls over.

His friend asks, "Mike, what are you doing?"

Mike, huh? Well let's see how you like this, Mikey. I turn and focus on his weakest point. Mikey hits the floor in the fetal position and screams. His friend's eyebrows crumple as he turns to look at me as if I'm the beast. I close my eyes and breathe slowly, counting backward just like the counselors taught me.

Mike backs up and screams at Shay, "What is he!

She answers, "He's the prince."

Everything stops, and I mean everything.

I can hear my own breath. Something moves in front of me. My eyes pop open to see Mike and his buddy bowing at my feet. Mike lifts his eyes. "I'm sorry, Prince. I did not recognize you."

Only one response I can think of, laugh.

BUT CURIOSITY

THE MUSIC BUMPS up. People make their way back to their party stances while the two guys stumble out of the room arguing over whose fault it is. Well, history class will be a little awkward on Monday. I run my hands through my hair and rub the back of my neck. Shay steps in close and begins to dance around me, moving in ways that reveal her inhumanity.

"We need to talk."

I grab her hand and pull her away from the crowd. Every eye is on me. Hands reach out, patting me on the back, shaking my hand, or simply going for a high five. I smile, nod, and keep moving. You would think I just saved the world.

Someone bumps into me on my left. Shay's hand clenches mine. Then I hear a sound right behind me. I listen. It's a low rumble—no, a growl.

My lungs are taking this way too seriously, pushing me to walk faster.

A tall brunette steps in our way, swaying to the music. I try to maneuver around her, but she wraps her arms around my neck with my arm hanging out to the side still grasping Shay's hand. I look into the brunette's eyes. There's a pulsating yellow behind an orange shade, like cat eyes. Maybe they're contacts. I look for lenses, but there are no lines. She rubs her body against mine and arches her back. My stomach jumps.

I twist away from the brunette and turn to face Shay, pulling her into me like a shield to block the crazy girl, my heart racing. The brunette doesn't take a hint very well. She brings her hands up around Shay, but her fingers are not normal. They're long and sharp and covered in blood. A wave of nausea flows from my brain to my stomach. I try to push back, but two more girls block me in, pawing at my chest with hands that are transforming. Face to face, I search for anyone normal, but I'm lost in a sea of hybrids coming to life.

My cheeks start to burn. I back away and stumble over my own feet. A guy shoves me and calls me a couple of names, but I don't care. I just want to get out of here. Shay is still in the center of the room, dancing with the brunette. I'm shoulder to shoulder in a never-ending room of beasts, searching for a way out, but finding it hopeless.

I focus and call out to Canyon and Caylee.

Guys, I need your help. I'm at a party on Badazz Drive. Just get me out of here, and I'll explain everything!

I start mumbling every detail about the yard, bricks, vicious Chihuahua, and anything else I can think of that will help them find me as I try to find a corner to disappear in.

Everyone is still having the time of their lives as if they don't notice what's happening all around them. Couples are making out, and most of the guys are slinging their drinks around and dancing with every girl possible. I finally back into the wall and stay there, hoping the twins will find me in one piece. How did I end up in this mess?

Maybe I can find a door and get out of here. I reach back to feel the wall but it's not a flat surface. It feels like...denim.

I turn and see a ginormous guy standing behind me. He's at least eight feet tall and covered in brown hair. His eyes are closed and he's not moving.

Slowly...step away from the Sasquatch.

I carefully move forward to get off of him, but two girls bump into me, knocking me backward. Of course, I bounce off of his rock-hard abs. No wonder I thought he was a wall. The hibernating beast awakens and glares right at me. His teeth break through his huge lips as he releases a grumble from deep inside that I can hear over the music. I apologize over and over as I back away, trying to escape.

His agitation has a domino effect on the happy crowd. All around me, low rumbles vibrate the room. The average height increases to at least a foot over my head. My shoulders drop.

Something slithers under the beasts' legs. I turn to see, but it moves too fast. A hand taps my shoulder. I jump and twist to face a beautiful creature, Shay. Her face is glowing. I look her up and down. Her clothes are covering just enough skin to leave room for the imagination to take over.

She bats her eyelashes. "It's almost midnight. Everyone is ready to celebrate the final leap year with our prince." Final?

Someone grabs my shoulders and yells, "It's time to parrrrrtay!"

My reflexes spin me around to face Levi. He smiles and puts his fist out for some sort of secret handshake. Of course Levi adds an extra punch, slide, jazz fingers, and a fancy ending complete with a shoulder bump. I ask, "How did you get back in here? I saw them drag you out."

He erupts with laughter. "Dude, really? They weren't taking me out! That cougar took me to the best poker game ever."

I shake my head. This guy is crazy. "So where's your boys?"

"Pssssh, they're around here somewhere. I'm sure they'll be fine." Levi pumps his eyebrows at Shay as if they have an inside joke.

Shay rolls her eyes and grabs my hand. "Come with me."

I look back at Levi. He's laughing and sending a double thumbs up. Shay jerks me forward to the platform where the DJ is seated. Next to his table is an oversized gold chair with a tall back and big arms facing the crowd. Shay smiles as if she just led me to courtside seats at a Mavericks game.

She lets go of my hand and motions toward the chair. "All you have to do is take your throne." Then she does the unexpected. She bows.

The entire room echoes her movement until they're all facing the floor. The music is still pounding against my chest. My heart can't take much more. I'm not ready to choose. My entire body starts to tremble.

Caylee, Canyon, please get me out of here!

I hear a laugh, but it's very close to me, too close and familiar. He's in my head isn't he?

Canyon laughs again and replies, *Hold up, bro, almost there.*

I yell back at him, *I don't have a second!*

I can see the door. It's across the room by the bar. No problem, there's only a hundred gigantic beasts blocking the exit. Where's the fire marshal when you need him?

I step up on the platform and look all around the room. In the back, a group pushes toward the front. Beasts roar, covering the sound of faint cries. Two guards carrying swords finally break through the crowd, pushing a dozen or so humans through the beasts and toward the throne, *my* throne. Beasts start moving and bouncing. The group of teenagers are now trembling and darting their eyes from beast to beast.

Shay is suddenly beside me and whispers in my ear, "These are empty souls. They will soon belong to the dark."

My heart is leaping. Belong to the dark?

The beasts back up, opening a circle in front of the throne. The guards push the teens into the circle. A few girls huddle together, crying. Obviously, this is not the leap party they expected. Two guys are whispering as if making plans to run for it. One tall guy steps forward. Steven!

His voice quakes, but he still speaks, "Prince, I choose to be your loyal servant." Then he drops to a knee and bows.

Shay nudges me with her elbow. "Watch this."

One of the guards walks over to him with his sword raised. Our eyes meet. The guard smiles back at me. I catch a glimpse of his face under his helmet. It's Aaron. I can't watch, but I can't look away. Steven stays down, looking at the floor. Aaron flexes and swiftly drops the sword toward Steven's neck.

I close my eyes. What's taking the twins so long? My eyelids turn an unusual shade of dark black. I open my eyes and immediately see the cause coming straight for me with a disappointed glare, the Hollow Man. He floats into me without knocking me down.

We are one.

Prince, you can either take souls or save souls. Lift your chin.

I follow his orders and look across the room at the sea of beasts.

This is your throne and these are your people. They kneel before you, willing to die to enter your kingdom, and you close your eyes!

I look at Steven. The sword clangs to the floor after slicing through his neck, but his head doesn't roll. A Troglodyte has attached to his back, protecting him from the blade. Steven sighs, and his eyes glimmer. He knows what just happened, and he's proud to have become part of the dark kingdom. He lifts his eyes to me and nods his head in subservience.

Then I see the same sparkle in every eye across the room until I see the eyes of the empty souls, begging. Begging for mercy, *my* mercy.

The time for you to choose is near. The decision will not wait until you're ready.

My chin wants to drop, but I force it to stay in place. My eyes want to close, but I stare straight ahead.

I know what I have to do.

A loud pop shakes the fireplace, exploding hot embers and ash all over the room. Beasts scream and scatter away from the brick wall. My chest heaves, the Hollow Man is on the floor next to me. The room looks like the epicenter of an aerial bomb zone. No one's left standing. Then I see three bodies walking through the fire as if the extreme heat did not affect them at all!

I recognize Canyon's voice from within the ash, "Johnny, you in here?"

Caylee huffs, "Well, if he is, then he and everyone else knows we're here too. Just go, big mouth!" I see her slug him through the gray wall of debris.

Canyon doesn't pay attention to her assault as he stomps out of the ash. Beasts are wiping their eyes and coughing soot out of their lungs all around him. Complete chaos takes over as they regain their ability to see. Some are running, others are angry and looking for the intruder.

Caylee rushes to my side. "I knew this was the place!" She cuts her eyes to Canyon who shrugs.

Canyon tries to smooth things over. "Let's just focus on the fact that we found him, okay?"

Beasts are back on their feet and they're not happy. I try to find Shay through the cloud of ash. My legs feel weak. I see her blond hair sweeping in and out of the fallen. She heads toward the hallway. A surge of energy sends me off the platform and running after Shay.

Canyon grunts, "He didn't even say hello."

Caylee slugs him and runs behind me. I can feel her warmth on my heels, but I feel someone else alongside me, the Hollow Man. Shay disappears into the bathroom, but I'm only a second behind her. She didn't shut the door all the way, enabling me to grab it just in time to see Shay step into the floor-length mirror by the window. Without a second thought, I follow even though the twins are screaming for me to stop.

Each step feels like I'm squeezing through a thick gel wall. I stagger into a square empty room full of bright lights and white walls. No windows, no furniture, and definitely no Shay. I'm completely alone.

Shay's voice enters my head, "Look around, Johnny. This is your reflection."

All four white walls turn into water and drop like a curtain, flooding the room. Beyond the missing walls, I see a growing cell of thunderstorms bringing a wall of darkness right at me. I brace myself for the impact of the winds and cold rain.

Shay laughs out loud. "You're so unpredictable. I never picked you as a raging storm kinda guy. Maybe a summer shower, but not fierce enough for this!"

I ignore her play on words and focus on finding her location.

She keeps talking. "So, you started as a bright shiny light; pretty annoying if I might say so. But then you turn into a dark raging storm. That's hot." She takes a loud breath. "But what does that say about your future throne? Surely you aren't considering the light! You're meant for darkness. Just think of the fun we'll have."

The Hollow Man appears beside me, his voice hard to decipher from my own, "She has a point."

I try to focus in on Shay's energy and not waste time thinking about things that don't matter. She's close by me, I can feel her.

"Johnny, what if I could show you where your parents are and help you free them? Would you choose to stay with me?"

"Shay, quit playing games. If you know where they are, prove it."

"You know where they are. We all do, but it appears I'm the only one willing to help you. Where are your friends from the light now that it's time to go into the pit of Dunabi?"

The Hollow Man jumps on the opportunity to speak up, "You know she's right, they haven't been exactly supportive. Look around, where are they now?"

My mind is struggling to differentiate my voice from the Hollow Man's. "Shay, I don't have time for any more games. Either help me or take me back."

A door appears in front of me. "If you go through that door, there's only one way back."

"Will I find my parents?" I ask.

"Yes, you will find a lot of things." Shay's voice dips as if implying a hidden meaning.

I look around, speaking to the empty room. "Are you going with me?"

Shay appears in front of me and grabs my hands. "This is your journey, not mine. I will be waiting for your return." She leans forward and kisses me softly and slowly, sending my head into a spin.

She steps back, dropping my hands, and my body rocks. I'm so dizzy. The door in front of me opens. My heart punches against my ribs. I stumble forward, surprised to see green grass and trees through the opening, but then a fog rolls over the land, uprooting trees and destroying everything in its path. I try to back up, but a blue orb of light wraps around me and pulls my body to the door. I struggle to push against the doorframe. It's useless.

Caylee, Canyon, I can't fight the portal's current. I need your help!

My arms collapse. I brace my feet on the doorframe.

Seriously, guys, where are you when I need you?

The Hollow Man uses my voice, but his words. *When are you going to figure it out, Johnny? No one is ever going to be here for you.* His words are like a double-edged sword cutting straight through my core. I can't take anymore of this. Every ounce of my energy is burned.

I let go.

OPENS A DOOR

MY BACK IS struck, flinging me to the ground. I skid across the dirt and roll a few times before landing next to a large gray stone. My head and elbow are screaming. I push up, crunching leaves with each movement. An ancient black iron fence encloses weathered stone buildings, statues, and me. My eyes follow the fence to find the only gate is wide open. That's a relief. Next to me, I hear a moan and turn to see Canyon lying behind a broken stone.

He rolls over on his back with his arms spread-eagled. "That hurt."

I rub my forehead. "Seriously? Aren't you an all-powerful Celestial?"

He props up on his elbows. "Have you seen this human body I'm stuck in?" He sits up, flexing his huge muscles, acting as if they're pathetic.

Another voice startles me. "Canyon, you're like this, human or not."

Where did she come from?

Caylee continues, "We need to find the door-way into Dunabi." She starts rummaging through the debris.

I stand up and grab Canyon's hand to help him to his feet. "How did y'all get in here anyway?"

Canyon starts humming and hunting for the doorway as if he can't hear me.

Caylee rolls her eyes. "We came in the room right as you were being forced through the door. So, we jumped."

I throw one hand in the air toward Canyon. "So you're what hit me in the back!"

Canyon shrugs. "Sorry, I was trying to avoid plowing over you, but it all happened so fast."

Caylee laughs. "Johnny, haven't you figured out Canyon's kind of like a bull in a china closet."

Canyon breaks up the laughter. "Yeah, yeah. So where's the dark guy that was pushing you?"

I dust off my jeans. "What did you say?"

Canyon sees that I have no clue. So he explains a little more, "A dark *you* pushing the real *you* into the portal. Where is he?"

My head suddenly feels like I'm trying to push up four hundred pounds on squat. I start looking for the Hollow Man.

"He is *not* me and I have no idea where he is!" I look to Caylee for some support, but she's giving me the same look as Canyon. How could they say that I'm anything like the Hollow Man! My insides feel like they're going to implode.

I take a few steps back and trip over a stone. There's something etched on the flat side. I lean down and wipe off the dirt. Always Missed, Always Loved. For a moment, I'm completely frozen, staring at the words. My stomach feels like a brick slamming down into my gut. I lift my head and scan the area. Near the huge black iron gate stands tall weeds camouflaging more scattered broken stones. I feel sick. With quick, jerky steps, I back away. These are gravestones!

I spin around. My voice shakes, "Guys."

Next to the stone is a huge hole with wood pieces all over the ground. I swallow, but a huge knot stays in my throat. These graves are open, desecrated. I see Canyon standing next to an overturned casket, but that's not the only one. Remains litter the entire graveyard.

My body is frozen stiff. "I think we should get out of here."

Caylee nods as Canyon shivers. "This place gives me the creeps."

As soon as Canyon finishes speaking, we all hear the huge iron gate slam shut. I turn and look across the graveyard. The large metal brackets clank. I see the Hollow Man locking us in. I crack my neck from side to side. Let's do this.

I barrel toward the Hollow Man, determined to destroy him. Anger flows through me, increasing my speed and power. His voice, my voice, enters my mind.

You cannot destroy me unless you destroy yourself.

I slow down.

You can't control me!

The Hollow Man laughs as if he knows something I don't. My chest starts to hurt as if I've been punched in the ribs. There's no way. He's just blowing hot air. I can feel my heart racing as my skin trembles.

The Hollow Man speaks up, *You need to wake up, Prince. These two halfwits are worthless. Follow me. I can protect you and I know where to go.*

I speak back to him through my thoughts. *Yeah, I know where you need to go too.*

The Hollow Man doesn't take no for an answer. He flies straight for me. I brace myself for impact, but Canyon sees him and uses his lineman skills to deflect the Hollow Man's momentum. When

One Prince, Two Kingdoms

Canyon's light strikes against the Hollow Man's darkness, a sudden pain strikes my chest, and I fall to the ground. Caylee runs and kneels beside me. "Johnny! Johnny!" I roll onto my side and clench my chest. Caylee screams, "Canyon, wait!"

Too late. A violent vortex has formed above Canyon and the Hollow Man that extends from the sky to the ground, destroying everything in its path. The force of the wind threatens to pull me and Caylee in, but she moves into a protective position hovering over me, blocking the winds.

The Hollow Man screams, sending a barrage of sound waves that hits Caylee and knocks her into me. I silently scream as my guts threaten to implode. Canyon returns the sound with a deep roar that sounds like a clap of thunder, knocking the Hollow Man to the ground. The immense pain flows throughout my entire body. I roll back and forth, hoping for relief. Caylee grabs my shoulders, "Johnny, stay with me."

The vortex loses its power, and Canyon drops next to him on all fours. The Hollow Man jumps to his feet and runs. Canyon is right on his heels.

Caylee yells again, "Canyon, wait!"

He keeps running and yells back, "Why?"

"You just have to!" she demands.

Canyon stops on a dime and stares her down. "What are you saying, Caylee?"

"I don't know for sure, but if you kill him, I think it might kill Johnny."

I really don't understand it myself, but I know it's true, I can feel it. My body's starting to depend on the Hollow Man more than it depends on oxygen. The intensity of pain in my chest is relieved as the Hollow Man runs away. I push up to face the twins.

Canyon yells, "Can we at least follow him?"

I nod and climb to my feet. Caylee stares at me as if she disapproves. I don't make eye contact and start jogging across the graveyard, dodging stones. Caylee is quick to pass me, leaving Canyon in the back.

Canyon huffs. "Why can't a guy get a break every now and then?"

"Shut up, Canyon," Caylee spits out.

I pass Caylee. There are only a few feet between the Hollow Man and me. The closer I get to him, the more powerful I feel. I want more. I reach out to grab him, but he literally drops into the ground. I hit the brakes and look down.

Caylee yells exactly what I don't want to hear, "In the grave, Johnny!"

Inside the coffin is a pile of bones poking out from under the decay. I look around for another option. No such luck. I take a deep breath and jump as if I'm cliff diving into the lake. Much to my surprise, the ground gives way to a staircase descending into the dark. No turning back now.

With each step, my knees want to buckle.

Canyon's behind me mumbling over and over, "I hate the dark, I hate the dark."

Caylee smacks him on top of the head. "Get it together, bro!"

I stop at the bottom, searching for the Hollow Man.

We're standing below a ceiling of roots with a thick wall of black fog boxing us in. Canyon's eyes are darting all around and he's holding his arms like he belongs in an insane asylum.

Another deep breath, courage finds its way inside of my gut, and I take the first step through the veil of fog. My feet clunk onto a hard surface.

I'm standing on a bridge that crosses over a beautiful teal blue river. On the other side is an enormous oak tree with limbs reaching to the ground. I draw in a deep breath through my nose and exhale slowly from my mouth. My eyes narrow and focus on the glimmering drops of water falling down the outer edge of the canopy. They gently rain into the sparkling river that encircles the city like a moat surrounds its castle. There's a soft light glowing from inside the thick canopy. I want to see more. I walk across the bridge and enter the limbs. Each step leads me deeper into the canopy's forest of branches and leaves.

I feel eyes watching my every move. Something shakes the limb next to my head. I stop and look into the thicket. It's only a drop of water rolling across a leaf. I reach out to touch it, but the veins on the leaf move, revealing a pair of sad eyes staring back at me. I jerk my hand back. An extreme sadness overtakes my entire body. I watch as a tear forms in those eyes and rolls off of the blade, glimmering as it makes its way to the river. I can feel a million more desperate faces watching me as they weep. A tear falls onto my cheek from a leaf right above me. I feel heavy. Another tear hits me, knocking me to my knees. I grab a branch and try to pull myself up, but it's hopeless. I'm all alone. Everyone who has ever loved me is gone. I am deadly. It is too dangerous to love me. I lean back on the limbs and feel them wrap around me. I close my eyes and fall.

◌ᴍᴍᴏ

Something jerks my arms nearly out of their sockets as it pulls me through the limbs. Hopelessness fades. I force my eyes open and see Caylee and Canyon each dragging one of my arms. I take a deep breath and sigh.

"Look who decided to wake up now that we're here," Canyon teases.

Caylee looks down at me and drops my arm. "Good morning."

"What happened?" I ask.

"You were down for the count and we rescued you!" Canyon brags.

"We?" Caylee asks with a serious sarcastic undertone.

"Yes, *we!*" Canyon tries to defend himself, "I helped."

Caylee grumbles, "Yeah, after *I* saved him."

"Saved me from what?" I ask.

"The Tree that Cries," Canyon points up.

A huge canopy arches over my head, covering a bright city with tons of people rushing in and out of shops as if it's Black Friday. Caylee leads us onto the only brick road entering the city. Little old shops and monstrous high rises have obviously coexisted here for many centuries. My attention immediately runs to the bright lights flashing from the Jumbotron in the center of the main intersection. Images of overly happy people enjoying the great city flash across the gigantic flat screen.

We walk past upscale boutiques and cafes next to pubs and party-all-night clubs full of people running on full-throttle desire. Every employee looks like plastic mannequins with frozen smiles and stiff arms handing out whatever the people ask for. Everyone's eating, dancing, and drinking without any rules or limitations. Whatever they want, they take.

I look from street to street, searching for the Hollow Man as we make our way toward the center of the city. I look down a back alley to a club. A mass of thugs are poppin' bottles and forcing a guy to chug. Overhead, an army of drunks is leaning over a balcony, making bets and sending down more supplies to torture the guy. I step a little faster to get around the corner.

A tall building draws my eyes upward. The sky above is nothing, but thousands of branches twisted together from the tree overhead. Each branch bounces a different color of light around the city like the mirrors on a disco ball.

A dark shadow cuts through the branches and darts to the ground. Gotcha! The Hollow Man pushes through a group of people at the carnival entrance less than two blocks away. I focus on his movement. He weaves in and out of the crazy patrons and game hosts yelling out over the music, offering everyone a chance to win. He's moving toward the Ferris wheel at the end of a gigantic pier overlooking a swirling ocean. Darkness hovers over the water, obscuring the unusual motion of the waves. Although I can't see exactly what's making the water twist and turn, I can feel the impending doom. It's time to move.

I wave my arms for Caylee and Canyon to follow. The three of us run down a main street through the bright city until we reach the carnival. Shoulder to shoulder, we try to pass through a school of teens. They're laughing and drinking without a care in the world. How are all of these people so happy when right beside them darkness is forming? My thoughts freeze. I'm emotionally paralyzed, as if these people are sucking the life out of me.

A big guy trips into me, but instead of apologizing he grabs my shoulders. "Get out of my way," he yells, then pushes me into a group of girls. Like bowling pins, they all fall and I bounce off of them. Caylee grabs my arm, using the distraction to pull me through an opening. Canyon is close behind. I try to regain my footing, but stumble over absolutely nothing. When I look up, I see the Hollow Man entering a shop across from the Ferris wheel.

The darkness from the ocean is spreading to the pier, expanding right before my eyes. The source of light from the branches above dims as if a cloud covered the sun. The twins must be seeing the same thing. I find my feet and run down the street facing the darkness, dodging a few clumps of rude shoppers, and enter the little store. The bells clang against the glass door as it slams shut behind us.

The room is completely empty. No cashier, no patrons, no Hollow Man. There's nothing to look at except rows and rows of new and old books. Caylee holds her finger up to her lips and stares at me.

I hear her speak inside my head. *I'll take the first row. You take the second, and Canyon the third.*

We all nod in approval and continue our search. The wooden floor creaks with each step. I keep one eye on the exit and my back to one side of the shelf. *I know you're in here and I know you're watching me. Show yourself.* A shadow passes overhead. *Well, crap, I didn't think about looking up.*

In slow motion, I lift my eyes to the ceiling. It's covered in old wooden screen doors. Behind each door is what appears to be normal humans smiling and waving for me to join them inside. Some are sweet old grannies and others are young guys laughing as if they are at a frat party. I force myself to focus and creep on.

My eyes dart above, below, left, and right. The shadow passes on my left and goes straight up the wall just like a cockroach scattering to hide. I jerk my head to see the Hollow Man staring at me from the ceiling.

"It's time." He smiles, sending chills down my spine.

The Hollow Man disappears behind a large wooden frame door with iron décor encircling the front. A middle-aged lady with a sweet smile looks down at me, motioning for me to come inside. I look up at the other doors to see each one inviting—no, begging me to enter their door.

I feel a surge of energy pass through me. Every one of my senses increases by a million. Before I see her, I can hear and smell Caylee approaching.

Caylee rounds the corner and walks up. "Johnny, it's midnight."

She grabs my arm and Canyon's. Within a second, we are in spiritual time.

Canyon slaps me on the back. "Happy birthday, bro!"

I RUSH IN

I FORCE A smile.

Caylee points up at the screen doors. "We'll have cake later. Right now you get to choose your first present, which passageway will it be?"

Now or never. I lift my head and scan the doors.

Nothing looks the same, as if my eyes were just opened for the first time. The normal humans peering out from behind screen doors have transformed into vicious beasts with blood and drool dripping from their fangs in anticipation of another meal. They're banging their heads against the doors and trying to rip the screens off so that they can feed.

As I pass underneath each door, I hear a growing screech from behind me like caged chimpanzees. There's no time to look back. I know exactly where I'm going.

When I pass the door with the party guy, he yells, "Hey, douche, what the hell is your problem? You think you're too good to join us in here?"

I refuse to look at him and keep walking. The old lady smiles her toothless grin as I approach, but the moment I step past her, she's enraged. She hits the screen door with all fours and slams her body against it, causing the ceiling to jolt with her movement as she screams. The pitch makes me wish I could close my ears. I reach the door with the smiling lady and look up at her.

She greets me, "Welcome home, my prince." Then she disappears.

A staircase drops from the ceiling. I step up toward the door and grab the handle. It opens too easily. A gust of air wraps around me, surrounding me with a high-pitched laughter that could peel paint off of the walls. Complete disorientation incapacitates my abilities. The sweet smiling lady's face begins to form in the wind, laughing at me. The force of air increases, making it impossible to breathe. Nothing is what it appears to be. I hold my breath and clench my fists, focusing all of my energy on the lady's eyes. Anger manifests inside of me.

I let go.

Darkness wraps around her face and presses her features together until her bones break. The lady's laugh spreads thin and increases in pitch. She's now screaming in pain. The wind releases me and follows her as she attempts to escape its power, vanishing into nothing.

My feet are planted on the floor, but a deep blackness blindfolds my eyes. I reach out and feel around until I find a wall, but this time, I make sure it's an actual wall.

I try to contact the twins telepathically. *Hey, guys, not sure where I'm at, but hopefully you do.*

Sit still, I'll find you. Caylee sounds like an annoyed babysitter.

I lean back on the smooth, cold stone. Curiosity attacks. I stoop down, following the curves until I find the floor. It's also a smooth stone, but covered in a layer of dirt, or at least what I hope is dirt. This must be their underground cave system. I stand back up and move along the wall, feeling for any more clues.

Marching feet approach. The hair on the back of my neck vibrates. I stand still and listen, wishing I could see. The marching stops. Someone bangs on a metal door three times. My muscles twinge with each hit.

The door creaks open, spilling light into the cave's hallway. "What the hell took you so long? Get your asses in here."

They leave the door propped open, shining a ray of light right on the cave walls behind me. The ceilings are a low, smooth stone that curves down to the cave floors as if this was once a water passageway eroded by the strong force of a river. As I move into the shadows, I look up and down the tunnel. There's no end in sight. The guards' voices stream into my ear, changing my focus.

One guy says, "Drake, check out my new blade."

"Cool, Brandon. Where'd you get that?" Drake asks.

"Yeah, Gaven, where did I get it?" Brandon replies.

Gaven grunts, "Off one unlucky gringo." Then I hear metal sliding against a stone. They're sharpening blades. My back wants to melt into the stone wall.

Another guy suggests, "Brandon, shouldn't we be on guard?"

"On guard from what, Chris? You worried your momma is gonna be mad if you don't do your job right?" Brandon taunts Chris.

"Shut up, Brandon. Let's go," Chris orders.

A different voice says, "Guys, we're wasting time. We need to get to our next checkpoint."

"Right, Derek, the *checkpoint*. You mean the check-her-out point?" harasses Brandon. They all laugh, and then Brandon says, "We better hurry before someone else gets to her first." He suddenly stops laughing and orders, "Let's roll."

No one argues. I hear obedient marching feet follow him out of the room and down a hallway. The other three guys stay in the room, laughing and making fun of Chris's momma. I feel faint. Then I realize I haven't been breathing. I force myself to relax and take a quiet breath.

A warm gust of air blows against the back of my neck, the smell horrid. I clench my fists and prepare to fight whatever this thing is.

Then I hear a whisper, "This is our chance, divide and conquer." Instantly, I recognize the voice. I'm so happy to see Canyon, but so grossed out. The boy needs a Tic Tac.

Caylee nods her head. "Johnny, you stay in the middle. Canyon, take the left flank. I'll go right. No prisoners."

My eyes feel like they're about to explode. Did she really just say no prisoners? Harsh. We all three fist pump and follow each other like a genuine SWAT team. Caylee holds her hand up, we stop and listen to the guards.

"Dude, turn up the volume. That chick's hilarious," a deep voice carries throughout the cave.

A squeaky voice answers, "Hold up. Why did they put so many knobs on this thing? Aren't we in the twenty-first century?"

"Move over, all you gotta do is twist that one and push her cell. Trust me, she's ridiculous." The one with the deep voice laughs.

We hear someone bang on a counter followed by the deep voice, "Dammit, nothing ever works for me. Reset the mainframe, again."

"No, you do it. I'm not touching nothing. Brandon will take my head," squeaks the guard.

Heavy footsteps cross the room. Then the deep voice orders, "Hey, Tic, wake up." We hear slapping and then a dark grumble.

"What the hell, guys? Take care of it yourself, you lazy assholes." The new voice is not amused. It sounds like he rolls over, followed by heavy breathing.

We hear the squeaky voice bounce around talking and running at the same time, "Funny you callin' us lazy, sleeping beauty."

The two guys start laughing and snorting at their lame joke. The third guy is not so humorous. "I will crack your skulls if you don't shut the hell up."

The laughter stops.

The banging on the counter returns.

"Move over, I got this," squeaks the guard.

After a few more clicks, we hear a female voice, "It's all my fault. Nothing I do is ever good enough. Not even good enough for the prince."

The two guys start slapping each other. The deep voice brags, "Dude, I told you she's ridiculous. Like the prince would ever like a halfwit like her."

The other one laughs and heightens his squeaky voice to sound like a girl, "He will never love me."

Laughter busts out, but is interrupted by an irritated third wheel. "I swear you two better shut it or I will break both of your jaws!"

The soft female voice is all that can be heard, "If only I was stronger, faster, prettier. Johnny, I'm sorry I left without you."

My heart hits the floor. I grab my chest and look at Caylee. Her face says it all. I'm ready to be harsh.

Before another word is spoken, we charge in the room.

The floor is like a maze made up of three-foot-tall ridges from dried-up cave pools weaving back and forth like ribbon candy. The flat surfaces are used as desks like the ones in a space station command center. There are huge screens hanging on every wall showing the never-ending hallways of cells throughout the cave. The main screen is focusing in on one cell with a girl curled up in the corner, rocking. Her beautiful black curls and olive skin are a straight giveaway, Danielle. I feel so many emotions—sorrow, empathy, hurt, love, anger.

Caylee jumps over the first row of desks and charges the biggest guy head on. She lifts his hunchback off the floor and body slams him tusk first into the floor before he knows what's happening. He lets out a deep moan, but gets right back up and charges at her like an angry boar. Caylee is swift. She moves slightly to the side and pushes him into one of the computers on the desk. His tusks smash into the screen, sending glass everywhere. He backs out and spins, catching Caylee off guard. The impact sends her flying down the aisle, knocking over every chair in her path.

Canyon moves like the wind. He's standing behind the other guy unseen. Canyon taps him on the shoulder. The guard jumps and squeaks. Canyon's fist greets him in the jaw, laying him out flat. With catlike reflexes, the skinny guy leaps to his feet with his hands on the floor and stares Canyon down. He twists his head and disappears. Canyon turns and looks all around the room. Without warning, the pale creature leaps over a row of desks and lands on Canyon's shoulders. Canyon grabs him with one hand and rips his claws out of his shoulders as he slams him against the wall. The skinny man moves fast and his claws are like razor-blades, slicing through Canyon's skin.

The final guy, my guy, has huge black wings with a chest bigger than the desks. Black leather and multiple swords cover him from head to toe. He rolls over on his makeshift bed and mumbles something about ripping their skulls off of their necks. I grab my neck. Johnny, pull it together. *You are the prince.* I nod my head as if giving myself permission. I look straight at him and allow my anger to flow through my veins. With focus, I project the rage toward the beast.

I let go.

The man stiffens up as if being electrocuted and convulses in his row of chairs. He growls and grits his teeth. With each second of pain, the man's growl increases in strength. In less than a minute, he overtakes the entire room with his piercing scream. Everyone falls to the floor except me. I stand there and watch him rise. I'm amused.

I let him go. He stands nine feet tall with wings stretching almost eight feet wide. The blades at the end of each feather sound like a sword being unsheathed as he extends them toward me.

Every muscle in his body is flexing. "How dare you use dark magic on me. Say your name or die." He clenches his jaw and stares me down.

I'm not afraid. In fact, I feel empowered. "How dare *you* rise against your prince. Bow." I point to my feet.

He cocks his head. "You are just a boy."

Not the right answer. Fury electrifies within me. My body jolts and the warrior falls to the floor. I feel...strong. I look down at my arms expecting huge muscles to pop out, but everything looks the same. I turn to see how Caylee and Canyon are doing, but they're all staring at me with mouths wide open. Canyon is holding the cat guy by the neck, and he's not fighting anymore. The boar is under Caylee's feet, motionless.

I look at them and tilt my head. "What?"

Canyon drops the cat dead to the floor. "What was that?"

I shrug my shoulders. "He shouldn't have called me a boy."

Canyon chuckles a nervous laugh. "Let's just hope you don't get mad at us."

I laugh back a bit too loud. The twins follow along, but I can hear a twinge of fear. Not a fear of me, but a respectful fear.

It doesn't take Caylee long to snap out of it and start ordering us around again. "Okay guys, y'all find disguises and I'll work on the mainframe."

Canyon stomps around the room opening every drawer.

I walk over to a closet. "Canyon, you really think a disguise will be in a desk drawer?"

He opens another drawer. "Could be, look." He holds up a pair of glasses with only one lens.

"Nice." I open the closet and find two more doors. "Should I pick what's behind door number one or door number two?"

Caylee turns and looks. "Don't open anything!"

Too late, I chose door number one. The moment I open it, alarms sound all around us. Lights are flashing and the door we came in slams shut.

"My bad." I give a cheesy grin.

Caylee glares at me like I'm her little brother who just broke her favorite doll.

Not good.

Canyon puts the glasses on. "Looks like we better hurry."

Caylee mumbles, "Hello, Captain Obvious." She rolls her eyes and keeps working on the computer.

I stand there with my hands out and peer inside the door. It's empty. Why would an alarm sound for nothing? Unless there's something hidden. I lean forward to look inside the closet. Something grabs me and jerks me backward.

"Johnny, do you really think sticking your nose where it doesn't belong is a good idea?" Canyon looks at me like I just fumbled the ball.

"I guess not."

"Might as well open door number two," Canyon grabs the handle and opens a closet full of black leather uniforms. He does his famous touchdown dance and grabs a couple, shoving one at me. I start slipping the black suit on over my clothes.

Caylee is frustrated. "This mainframe is a non-stop system that is lock-stepping the instructions across the mainframe. I need to isolate the functioning processor in order to divert the instructions and override the entire system."

Canyon looks at me and I look at him. Our eyebrows are up and we both shrug our shoulders. We have no idea what she's talking about. I finish putting the leather uniform on over my clothes. The flashing alarm lights are still screaming at us every two seconds. Canyon grabs a few swords and goes over to Caylee.

"Here, you need to put these on. Let me have a go at it." Canyon smiles at Caylee. She knows he's right, but also knows he doesn't have a clue about computer processing. She hops up and dresses faster than any runway model. Canyon starts playing whack-a-mole on the keyboard. Suddenly, water starts spraying from the sprinklers on the ceiling.

"Canyon!" Caylee screams.

"Oh no, I would hate for you to get wet, my pretty. You might melt." Canyon teases her as he continues slapping buttons.

"Just stop. I'll fix it in a sec." Caylee is hopping around trying to put the boots on.

I walk over to Canyon. The computer is flashing multiple warnings. I reach over the keyboard and hit the escape button. The sprinklers stop. Canyon reaches out for knuckles. When he does, he drops the keyboard. It smashes into the central processing unit. Sparks fly. We jump back and fall over the chairs. The lights dim and the entire computer system shuts down. The doors open and a low red light flashes throughout the room.

"See, I told you I would fix it!" Canyon brags as he crawls back to his feet.

"Yeah, you made it a whole lot better." Caylee looks at the computer screen. "You actually disabled the system, but it won't last forever. We'd better get out of here before it finishes resetting." Caylee runs for the door.

We follow without question and start moving down the dark hallway. Behind us, we hear soldiers marching into the control room. For now, they're distracted.

We rush to the end of a stone hallway and enter a large gathering room. Rows and rows of stadium seats are facing the front of the room where a huge stone table sits. To our far left and far right, I notice two hallways leading out of the room.

I elbow Canyon. "Door number one or door number two?"

"I don't like that game." Canyon lowers his eyes and glares.

I silently laugh at him.

Caylee ignores us and starts thinking out loud, "According to the map in the control room, it should be the door to the left."

Multiple footsteps and loud voices approach from across the room. The three of us slump back against the wall and wait to see what's coming.

TO SAVE THEM

A GROUP OF disfigured humans wearing long robes enter the room quietly and sit on the front row. Then the screaming begins. Tall, slender beasts with cat-like movements drag a woman with small hands and beady eyes into the center of the room and hold her up next to the table. She rubs her hands together and wipes her face a million times per second. A large man with broad shoulders and six eyes enters, announcing the woman's failures. Then without a trial, they sentence her to a lashing. She covers her face and screams.

Two guards chain her to the table facing up. A man the size of a grizzly bear with lizard-like eyes and scaly skin emerges from the corner covered in armor. He's carrying whips with sharp pieces attached to the end.

Time to choose a hallway and get out of here. We act like we're on assignment as we skim around the room and slip down the hallway to the right. No one in the room even notices us walk through; they're too excited to watch the lashing.

A few yards down the hall, there's an opening with a giant cave column dividing the passageway into two more halls. We cross a stone bridge overlooking another large gathering room where a second ceremony is about to begin. This time, I don't look, but the screams paint a disturbing image that will be forever etched in my mind.

Once across the bridge, we come to an opening higher than any mountain above ground covered in long, curving stones weaving beside one another: a petrified waterfall. We hike around a large boulder and find three more openings in the cave wall. This place is crazy.

"What now, sis?" Canyon whispers.

Caylee shrugs her shoulders.

I whisper what I think is the obvious choice. "We split up. Three halls, three of us."

Canyon's not so sure. "You first."

I roll my eyes. Thanks, Canyon. I choose the first hall.

Canyon doesn't wait long before I hear him in my head, *Yo, Johnny, if you need anything, just holla!*

I wish there was a telepathic "like" button. Instead, I reply with a simple, *Okay.*

The hallways are in a twisted maze design, turning every direction. Then I see cells up ahead.

I tell the twins, *So far, no guards, but I see plenty of cells. I'm pretty sure the coast is clear.*

Canyon replies, *There is a big difference between pretty and not, Johnny.*

You're a funny one, now get moving, I tell him.

Someone's feelin bossy! Canyon gripes.

I hear Canyon grunt and Caylee laugh. She must have hit him again.

We've been walking for a few minutes when cries from deep within echo in my ears. Hundreds of people are moaning and crying. I stay against the wall and advance toward the sounds. Somehow I know my parents and Danielle are trapped somewhere in there.

In my head, I hear Canyon ask Caylee and me, *Do you both hear what I hear?*

Caylee answers, *Yeah, wait until you see it.*

I continue until I reach an arched entryway. I look through and see what appears to be hundreds—no, thousands of rows of jail cells. This place is a never-ending abyss consumed in misery and darkness. The stone walls make me feel as if I'm in a medieval castle headed straight into the heart of the dungeon's torture chamber. As I approach the first cell, I see a woman in the corner, rocking back and forth as she cries and clings on to her necklace. The cell is a plain cave dug out of the stone with dirt floors and no bars to hold her inside, but she doesn't attempt to leave.

I ask the others, *Do the cells have bars in your hall?*

Nope, answers Canyon.

Sad, they could leave anytime they want to yet they choose to stay, Caylee adds.

Then why do they stay? I ask them.

It's all about choices, Johnny. They choose to believe they are trapped. And what you believe becomes part of you. It can either give you power or take it away. These people have made their choice, Caylee explains.

So if they change their minds, they can just get up and walk out of here? I ask.

Yep, the truth can set them free! Canyon exclaims.

I pass cell after cell full of people who believe they're trapped, but all they have to do is believe the truth and go free. Such a simple solution, I don't understand why so many are here if it's so easy. I pass multiple rows until I see long, dark curls. I stop and listen to her sweet voice as she repeats, "I failed. Everyone's gone because I failed." It's not her fault. I have to make this right.

I yell to the twins, *Found her!*

Caylee replies, *What cell number?*

I find a number etched in the archway. *6426.*

Danielle's body is moving back and forth at a rapid pace. She's facing the wall and mumbling, "It's all my fault, all my fault."

I want to hold her and tell her how sorry I am. My heart races. What if she hates me, forever?

An electronic sound fills the hallway like a computer booting up. A pressure presses against my skull. I grab my ears and shut my eyes, kneeling to the floor. I duck and cover. Rocks fall from above raining on my back. It feels like an earthquake shaking the floor and then I hear a loud boom. I wait a second. Everything is still again. I lift my head and look around. Prisoners act like nothing happened. I turn to look at Danielle, but she's gone. I run into her cell.

Guys, did you feel that? Canyon asks.

Yep, the cells moved. Caylee acts like she knows everything.

Danielle's gone! They took her! I clench my fists and look around her cell.

Where are you, Johnny? Caylee asks.

In her cell! Where else would I be?

Johnny, step out and look at the number again. Caylee makes me focus.

I look up. My eyes bug out and I yell inside my head at Caylee, *5426! What the heck?*

She explains, *Danielle's room was in the 6000's. So, the cells shifted up. Time to climb, and fast before they move again.*

Caylee's right. Everything may look the same, but the numbers are completely different.

I run to the end of the hall and dart up the staircase. I find 6426. Danielle is still sitting in the corner, not even fazed by the damage from the earthquake. I'm not losing her again. I jump inside her cell.

Danielle doesn't appreciate my intrusion and jumps at me like an infected zombie, screaming as she clutches the medallion dangling from her necklace. "My parents are dead because I failed! It's too late! Too late!" Then, like a seriously mental patient, she retreats to the corner, curls up, and starts mumbling again, "I failed, I failed" over and over as she rocks back and forth, still clinging on to that frickin' medallion.

Without a second thought, I grab the medallion and jerk it out of her hands, ripping it off of her neck.

Danielle screams, "Why did you do that?" She leaps up and charges at me.

Why *did* I do that? The medallion is burning my hand, but I refuse to let go. With one hand, I grab Danielle's shoulder and hold her back. She screams obscenities at me and flails around like a toddler having a tantrum. I stare into her eyes, hoping she'll come back to me.

Danielle's face is changing, changing into a beast full of rage. "Give it back! It's mine!" She claws and hits at me. "I want to go back. I'm happy inside there, not out here! Let me go back! Give it to me!" She falls to the floor and covers her face, crying. "Give it back."

I sidestep around her and back into the corner to get a better look at the medallion. What's the deal with this thing? In the center is a leaf, but deep inside there's movement. I focus and see the flashing lights from the dark city and all the people enjoying complete fulfillment of their unrestrained desire. Then I remember the sad eyes in the leaves, the water drops falling from the leaves, the glimmering waters surrounding the city. Could the water be the prisoners' tears falling from these medallions? I look at the person in the cell across from Danielle. He's rocking and crying in the corner, clutching his medallion.

My hand burns more with each passing second. I look down; the medallion's glowing and getting hotter. I can't hold on to it anymore. I let go. Danielle scrambles to catch it, but I leap toward her and wrap her up in my arms. Before it hits the dirt, particle by particle, it vanishes into thin air.

Danielle buries her face in my chest and cries. I hold her trembling body.

She whispers, "They're dead."

"How do you know that for sure?" I ask.

"I saw them thrown into the waterfall and watched my parent's bodies float away into the Black Sea. I should have done something. I should have saved them." Danielle quietly sobs.

"Danielle, you did all that you could." My voice feels thick. "It's not your fault."

I should have gone with her. Maybe they would still be alive. I drop my chin to her head, trying to embrace and protect every part of her.

She cries.

I hug her tightly against me.

Caylee and Canyon run in to Danielle's cell at the same time. Canyon grabs Caylee's arm and pulls her back. "Maybe we should give them some space." He winks at me.

Caylee jerks her arm free. "Canyon, you're such a twit sometimes."

"It's okay, guys." I push Danielle back and look into her eyes. "Danielle, we need to get you out of here."

She shakes her head. "No, I can't leave without my parents!"

"You're not leaving them. Staying here will take you away from them forever." I know she hears me, but her eyes are ready to fight.

"I was with them until you barged in here and took them away from me!" Her entire body lights up with anger.

My hands drop to my side. She's talking out of her head.

Caylee butts in, "Danielle, that wasn't real."

"Yes, it was! Shut up, Caylee, you don't know anything!" Danielle screams.

Canyon's eyebrows almost fly off the top of his face.

Caylee pumps her fists, but somehow holds herself back.

I jump back in, "Danielle, I found you in this cave. You were not with your parents!"

"Yes, I was! We were at home, and I was sitting next to dad watching TV. Mom was talking about our vacation plans to the mountains. We're going skiing in two weeks!"

I take her hands. "Danielle, you were in that corner, rocking and holding onto your necklace."

She freezes. "The medallion."

I squeeze her hands. "It had you under some kind of spell, but now you're free."

Caylee adds, "Free right now, but if we don't get you out of here, we will all be captives."

Canyon shivers. "I think we should go now and talk later."

Danielle's eyes are vacant. "Okay."

"Okay, she said okay, let's go!" Canyon is a little too excited.

"Canyon, you get Danielle out of here," Caylee orders.

"Why me?" Canyon grunts.

"Because Johnny's the only one who can save his parents. We don't have time to argue, Canyon. Once Danielle leaves this cell, the guards will know and attack her again. You're the strongest, so get her home." Caylee may have been spitting orders, but her eyes are crying out in fear.

Canyon must have felt her weakness. "Fine, but you and Johnny go first. We will give you a head start. Remember, we don't have time to argue. Just go."

Danielle grabs my arm. "Wait, Johnny, your mom is in cell 216." She hugs me and whispers, "Please, come back. I can't live if I lose you too." She steps up on her tiptoes and kisses me on the cheek. Time stands still. My body fills with warmth. I stare into her icy blue eyes and wonder.

Caylee grabs my arm and jerks me back. I nod and run away from Danielle's cell and down the hall. I try to shake off the surge of desire. Focus, Johnny. Caylee came from the 200 block and knows right where to go. We run down a long hallway and turn to go down a huge staircase that's open to see everything above and below us. The people inside the cells don't even notice us running by as they're so consumed by their medallions. We come to the 200 block and run down the hall. I slow to a jog and pass 213, 214, 215, 216! I stop and look inside.

It's empty. The dirt-covered floors show marks of a struggle, like someone has been taken out of the cell against their will. I follow the drag marks down the hallway. Caylee doesn't say a word. We come to the stairs where the marks end.

I look at Caylee. "Which way, up or down?"

She shrugs her shoulders and remains quiet. I have to make a quick decision. My instincts take us down the stairs. We pass the 100 block and go down one more floor. We're at the bottom underneath all the cells. The extreme heat increases along with the rotten smell. This is worse than the boy's locker room inside our field house. I check out the cave all around me before making any sudden moves.

The room is large with the same stone walls and dirt floors. There are six tunnels leading away from the main room. A high-pitched siren sends a sudden tidal wave of sound, drowning out the screams followed by an explosion of synchronized footsteps. Suddenly, the empty room is not empty anymore. Soldiers are everywhere. Caylee and I back against the wall and stand perfectly still.

Soon we're shoulder to shoulder with these disgusting creatures as they grow in excitement. Their leader enters the room and speaks loud enough to be heard over all the noise. "Cell 6426 has been vacated. We have a hostile among us. You must quickly find her and take her to the dungeon."

As soon as he finishes speaking, the soldiers march in all directions. They know exactly what to do and are excited to begin the hunt. Their focus on the mission causes them to miss the fact that two "hostiles" are standing right beside them.

The room clears except for one unit of six soldiers. They're scouring the main room. It's obvious their vision isn't 20/20. Caylee and I move into the first tunnel, escaping the main room. We find another cave with a table in the center and chains on the wall.

"Caylee, this looks just like the room in my dream." I point to the chains. "That looks just like the wall my dad was chained to. There have to be more rooms like this close by. Come on." I run out of the room. Caylee is right behind me.

We try to find connecting tunnels that lead to more torture rooms. We see things that should not exist. The creatures down here are more hideous than anything above. There are short, fat ones that move very quickly from room to room. Extremely large beasts are posted in each torture room. Occasionally, they're in the process of torturing a human or one of their own. As we continue deeper into the tunnels, the screams get louder and never stop. What if that's my parents screaming? My guts tremble, but I keep running.

"Johnny," Caylee says, gasping for air. "Johnny, we should go back."

She may be scared, but I don't have time for that. I ignore her, but slow down to give her a chance to catch her breath.

"Johnny, please! Something isn't right. We can come back later," she pleads.

I shake my head and keep moving.

I should've listened to Caylee. A group of six soldiers march down the tunnel heading right for me. Caylee grabs my arm and motions for me to be quiet. Her subtle movement was just enough to catch the attention of the tallest guard. He stops, and the other five stop with him. They all turn their heads at the same time like some kind of alien species and look in our direction. There's nowhere for Caylee and me to hide.

We run.

Caylee yells through her deep breaths, "Johnny, we have to get out of here!"

"Go ahead. I'm not leaving without my parents!" I scream back.

Together, we run down another tunnel and duck into a small room with a low ceiling. Something smells disgusting in here like a pile of horse crap. I grab Caylee and push her into a tiny cave in the far corner. We're still breathing heavy, but trying to be quiet as the soldiers approach. Their footsteps slow down outside of the room. After a long pause, marching begins again and carries the six soldiers away.

I feel a sensation of relief followed by a warm rush of air on my shoulder. I turn, expecting to see Caylee recovering and out of breath. To my surprise, I'm facing huge bull nostrils that are huffing in a slow, steady rhythm. It's too dark to see all of it, but I see enough. We back out of the cave, hoping we don't wake that thing up. And wouldn't ya know, the second we are safe, we bump into the three guards from the control room.

"Well, look what we have here, guys." I recognize his voice, Brandon. The other two laugh.

"Here, everyone is hunting hostiles, and we found them." Brandon actually thinks he's *The Man*.

The tall one named Derek is nodding. "We are good."

"What do you want to do with them, Brandon?" asks Chris.

"Maybe we should throw him in with his mommy and daddy. We could have a good ol' family reunion," Brandon taunts.

He knows where my parents are. "Where are they?" I yell and run toward Brandon, ready to knock him out. Chris surprises me and grabs my arm.

"Oooh, scary, isn't he?" Chris picks me up with ease and throws me against the wall, slamming my head against the stone. My body wants to pass out, but I'm too stubborn. Caylee jumps over to help me, which only increases their taunting.

They laugh at me while Derek suggests, "Why don't I take these two down to the dungeon so they can have some alone time?"

"Why would we let them be alone, I want to watch."

Brandon completely creeps me out.

"I can handle these two. You and Chris go get the other half of the family. Then we can enjoy dinner and a show!" Derek tries to take control.

Brandon's face is hard. He stares at Derek for a moment as if he is considering ways to kill him. Then, out of nowhere, he breaks into complete hysteria. "That sounds like a real treat. It's a party!" Brandon jumps and claps. Then his demeanor changes back to dark and angry. "You will get a taste of what your father has done to us."

He jabs me in the chest with his sharp ring, causing a stream of blood to soak through my shirt. I refuse to show weakness. I'm pretty sure Brandon's multiple personalities are all trying to speak at once and he's the one who needs some alone time.

Brandon slowly smiles. "I will enjoy watching the pain, *your* pain." He jerks his head toward Chris and growls in a deep, hoarse voice, "Let's go." They vanish around the corner.

Derek looks down on Caylee and me. "Get up," he orders.

Caylee stands first. I think about attacking Derek. He's just as huge as the guy in the control room with blades at the end of each feather. I know I can take him, but I need to wait until I'm a safe distance from the other guards. We follow Derek down the hall and into a small corridor.

He turns to us and whispers, "You need to go down this hallway and follow it until you come to a dead end. Take the stairs to your left and they will lead to the Tree that Cries. You know what to do from there." He turns and walks away.

A sudden coldness hits my core. What just happened here?

Caylee whisper yells, "Let's go!" and starts down the hall. I don't move.

She turns back. "Come on, Johnny."

Without a word, I turn the other way and follow Derek. Caylee runs back to me and tries to pull me in the other direction. I look at her. "No. I came here to get my parents, and I'm not leaving without them."

Caylee stops and backs against the wall. I know something's wrong. A warm rush of air goes down my back. Obviously, the bull's nostrils have returned.

FROM THEMSELVES

I TURN TO see an extremely large bull pawing at the ground. He pushes off the floor and rises onto his hind legs. His chest pumps out and he roars blowing saliva into my face. Dis. Gus. Ting.

I can't run, so I get down into my three-point stance and prepare to use every football play Canyon has taught me to stay alive. I wait for the perfect moment, and charge. We collide. The beast falls to the ground and rolls right back up. He's on all fours, growling and snorting. I push myself up and prepare to fight again. The bull runs toward me, I jump out of his way. He runs past me and slams into the cave wall. My heart leaps out of my chest. That was too close for comfort!

The bull turns around, pawing the floor. In a flash, he pushes off the wall heading straight for me. I twist and jump off of the wall, but I lose my balance and fall to the floor. The bull is fast. His hooves press into my back, pinning me to the floor. I cannot breathe.

The entire cave rattles. My hand hits something sharp and slices open. The scent of my blood causes the beast to lift off of me, raising his nose to smell the air. I grab the sharp object, twist over, and jab the stone into his neck. It easily slides through his thick fur and hide and into his jugular.

His blood spills.

The beast writhes in pain, snorting and slinging his head side to side. His nose hits my head and throws me across the floor, slinging blood all over me as he finally falls to the floor, moaning unnaturally.

Caylee runs to me, pulling me up. "We need to get out of here."

I groan and grab my head.

Derek is standing over me and reaches out as I grab his hand to pull up. A surge pulses from his body through mine as if I just chugged a five-hour energy drink, but better, way better. I feel like the Hulk.

The floor rattles followed by multiple angry bellows. Approaching hooves pound against the stone. The bulls move at an alarming rate. This is not going to be pretty. Derek motions for us to follow and runs down the dark hallway. I'm on his heels, but Caylee makes a wrong turn.

We're separated.

The bulls follow Caylee, and I'm in a new mess of my own—the other guards are back. Chris grabs my arm and heaves me into a dungeon, throwing me on the floor. I look up and see my dad chained to the wall. Right across from me is my mom, crumpled in the corner, rocking and mumbling while holding a medallion.

Without a second thought, I leap in front of her and grab the medallion. "Mom, I need you to let me take this."

Mom is crying, but she nods. I lift it off of her neck and watch it disintegrate into nothing. Mom's eyes return to normal and she gives me a long awaited smile. "I knew you would save me, son."

As we're smiling at each other, her body becomes transparent. I reach out to grab her, but it's too late. She turns into a vapor and disappears.

I panic.

What did they do with my mom? I look at my dad and he's smiling. What kind of sick game is this? The beasts are screaming and blaming each other for letting me get too close to her. My body loosens and I shake my head. Pull it together.

Crawling, I approach my dad, but a swift kick in the side from Brandon stops me from getting too close. "Not so fast, buddy. You may have gotten rid of your mommy, but we have big plans for you and your daddy."

I'm not going to let him hurt my dad. I stand to my feet. "Over my dead body."

Brandon laughs. "That can be arranged." Then he motions for Chris to attack.

Before I can blink, Chris slams me into the wall, and I fall to the floor. I refuse to give up. Slowly, I force myself back onto my feet.

Then I stare at Chris, anger manifesting inside me.

I let go.

A line of fire shoots across the room toward Chris. He wraps his wings around to block the flames, but the force of my fire knocks him to the ground unconscious.

Brandon exclaims, "Very good, Prince." He looks at Derek and motions for him to get my dad.

I run toward him, yelling, "Dad, fight! Take off the medallion, Dad! It's me, Johnny. I'm here!"

Brandon yells, "Silence!" The room shakes with the vibrations of his voice. I stop in front of my dad. Tears are streaming down his face.

"I'm sorry, son," he groans.

There's no medallion around his neck and I cannot break his chains. "It's okay, Dad. I love you."

I reach out to him, but something grabs my foot and slams me face first against the floor. Without giving me time to recover, it hauls me across the room. Fingernails digging deep into my skin, as it lifts me up and throws me on the table. The impact causes extreme pain in my skull. Warm blood oozes across my forehead. I try to open my eyes, but my vision is blurry. I can hear the whip with metal pieces clanging together as a large beast approaches me. I can hear my dad weeping and mumbling.

Brandon announces, "This is going to be the entertainment of the year!"

There's a flash and the sound of swords clashing. I hear Brandon yell, "Ray, you have no authority here!" Something picks me up and runs.

A sword slices the air next to my head making impact with whoever's holding me. From deep inside, they let out a painful groan. I blink my eyes and see Derek's face. His eyes are huge and staring back at me, struck with horror. He tries to take a deep breath, but his injured lungs can only handle a quick gasp.

His eyes drop in defeat. "I tried, Prince."

I feel every last bit of strength leaving his arms as Derek's grip on me releases. His knees buckle and we both hit the ground.

The impact slams my head against the stone for the last time. Everything is spinning, and then it all goes black.

᠃᠌᠌᠃

A beautiful female voice whispers words that give me power. I open my eyes. Although it is still black all around me, I can see clearly.

My dad is still on the wall, but he's not trying to escape. His head is down. I stand and walk over to him. He doesn't move.

The voice is next to me. "He's here because of his guilt."

I turn to see a woman wearing a black dress with a black crown covered in black diamonds, Queen Nara.

I ask, "What did he do?"

"He broke the treaty by entering Dunabi and setting captives free."

My eyes widen. "What makes that a crime? You're the one holding them against their will."

She smiles. "You have much to learn."

"Then tell me."

"We do not steal the captives, they come on their own accord. The shadows bring the ones who need to be here, and we protect them from the Light."

"Why would anyone need protection from the Light?"

"The captives are in a dark place trying to find their way. The Light has no tolerance and will execute judgment, exposing their shortcomings and scarring them for all to see. Light and dark cannot coexist."

"But the dark is evil."

"Johnny." She reaches out to touch my face and I flinch. Her shoulders drop and she looks down at her hands. "Just because something does not fit into the mold of perfection and normalcy does not make it wrong." She pauses and then looks up at me. "Different is not evil."

"Okay, then why are your Trogs trying to kill me?"

"No one is trying to kill you, but everyone is trying to lure you into their kingdom. You are the most powerful of all the Descendants. With great power comes the burden of responsibility. Only you can choose which kingdom you will reign over, and I promise no harm will ever come to you."

I believe her. Her green eyes fill with tears. She moves toward me and I almost want to embrace her.

She tilts her head. "You are strong and brave. I know you will make the choice that is right for you and your people."

She rubs her hands together and places her palms on my temples. A warmth spreads across my brain and down into my body. A memory tries to surface, but it's not strong enough. The warmth sizzles, giving me energy and strength above the normal human. I feel like a god!

⌇

I'm standing and Derek is lying lifeless on the ground at my feet. He would have been a great asset to my kingdom. So loyal, even to death. I bend down and touch his forehead, releasing his spirit to return to Shamayim, the City of Light. His remaining photons pulsate into my body.

I look around the room for Ray, but he's gone. The beasts are staring. My dad is still chained to the wall.

He tries to put on a brave face. "Son, it's time for you to go."

I crumple my brow.

He tilts his head. "I promise I will still be here when you get back." Dad tries to laugh, but starts coughing in pain. Our eyes lock, knowing this is not over. I put my hand on his shoulder and focus all of my energy, letting it flow into him. Three beasts rush toward me. Two of them grab my arms and sling me backward. I leap up and charge.

Dad stops me. "Son, you have to go while you can."

I look at him hanging there. I want to save him, but I know the time is not now.

"I will come back for you." I pull my arms away from the beasts and consider stomping their worthless heads into the ground.

A satisfied smile covers my dad's weak face. "I know you will." His eyes gleam as he heaves for air. I want to reach out and help him. Instead, I run out of the room, leaving him there weak and alone. My chest caves with each step. I force my mind to ignore my feelings and stay on course.

Caylee runs up the hallway, out of breath. "Johnny!" She stops in front of me. Her eyes scan me up and down. "You've changed."

"Not really." I shrug. "I guess you could say I just found myself." My dad's face flashes in my mind.

She smiles with admiration. "Much better." The red lights flash in the hallway, Caylee snaps back. "We should probably get moving. The system is about to reset the security defenses, which will make it impossible to get out of here."

"Let's move." I step past her and jog down the stone hallway and turn to pass through a tunnel that opens up to a large room. The lights are flickering back on to full strength. Hundreds of footsteps are gathering nearby.

Caylee's face confirms what I'm hearing.

I run into a small tunnel, taking us out of the large room and into a huge cave. It's cold and smells like an ashtray. I've smelled this before. Red hair and green eyes flash through my mind. I hold my arm out and stop Caylee from passing me. I put my finger up to my mouth to keep her quiet as I inch closer. The tunnel leads me to a huge, empty cave. Nothing. I shake my head and step inside with Caylee right behind me. My muscles ache from the extreme cold. Caylee tugs on my shirt. I turn to see her looking up with her mouth hanging open.

The cave's ceiling is covered, not in beasts but demons. Their chests pump irregularly as they hang there, lifeless. I glance around, wishing I could hit fast forward. There's too many for us to fight and we can't go back. I see a tunnel not too far from us. I motion for Caylee to stay close, hoping we can cross the room without disturbing the resting demons.

We stay against the wall and take one cautious step at a time. The guards' footsteps are getting close, bringing an army of dark beasts out to play. The tunnel opening is only a few yards ahead of us. We walk a little faster, keeping our eyes up. A group of guards pound their way into the cave. The demons shift. My stomach drops. Now or never! I grab Caylee's hand and run. An ear-piercing screech fills the tunnel followed by the sound of a thousand wings coming to life. There's no need to look, the demons are awake.

We run through two more halls, passing empty torture chambers until we reach the cave system of cells. The electronic sound shakes the floor and the cells shift. We cannot stop. We run down the hallway to the other side. The lights are flashing overhead with a siren blaring throughout the caves. The people inside the cells continue to rock and cling onto their medallions, oblivious. Weak.

We are near the control room. Ten more steps. A gust of rotting flesh fills my nostrils. The beasts are near. I hear clomping feet behind us. Then a crowd of guards appears at the far end of the tunnel running toward us. My arm is jerked into a cell just as the shift moves the rows. Caylee smirks like she just saved the day and is waiting for me to give her a cookie. I smile and hop out as soon as the shift stops. Caylee follows. We run down the hallway parallel to the floor below us and enter a tunnel. We are right above the control room.

I hear a rushing sound closing in all around us. We run around a corner and stop. In front of us is an active waterfall crashing thousands of feet below into a deep canyon. Behind us we hear the distant sound of guards searching for us. We've hit a dead end.

Caylee is losing her grip. "How are we going to get out of here?"

I look around the cavern, examining the walls. "There has to be more than one way to get above ground."

"Yeah, but we could end up in China if we take the wrong one." She leans back on the wall and tries to catch her breath. I'm not even winded. Cool.

I walk over to Caylee and lean against the wall. My hand slips on a ridge in the stone. I catch myself, planting both feet on the ground, and cross my arms as if I did that on purpose. Heat sweeps across the back of my neck settling into my cheeks. I avoid Caylee's eyes and look up to see what I slipped on. There's an eroded set of stairs in the bedrock. I unfold my arms and step closer. The opening above looks similar to the stairway that we used to get down here, but it's blocked. I look at Caylee and point up. "It's worth a shot."

We hear grunts and heavy feet closing in on us. She agrees. "Anywhere is better than here."

I climb to the top and reach up to push the rock out of the way, but it's happy right where it is and not willing to move. I balance myself and flex every muscle, pushing with everything inside of me. The rock slides out of the way enough for Caylee to pass, but I'm not sure I'll fit. I've just got to get her out of here before it's too late.

I smile as if everything is fine and motion for Caylee to use my hands as the first step. "Ladies first."

She doesn't say anything, but with one swift motion she steps on my hands and flies up and out. Once she moves out of the way, I jump and try to pull myself out. The stone is actually a ten-foot tall boulder. Caylee is standing above me, pushing against it. Her face is turning red.

I'm pushing from underneath the rock and trying to speak. "Caylee, get out of here."

She scowls and runs off.

Not what I expected. Caylee didn't even put up a fight; she just ran away and left me underneath a boulder with beasts on my heels. Next time, I should consider the consequences of my words. I push her to the back of my mind and focus on moving the boulder a few more inches. I moved it once. So I can move it again. I'm not about to give up. I manage to wedge my upper body out of the hole. With both arms and plenty of leverage, I close my eyes and push. The stone easily glides out of my way. I jump out of the hole. I can hear the

Trogs entering the waterfall chamber below. Time to put the boulder back.

I run to the other side and find Caylee already pushing. I let out a sigh and together, we push it back in place. We both turn around and slide to the ground leaning back on the boulder.

I look over at her. "I thought you left me."

Her lungs are heaving. She manages to say, "Like that will ever happen." She turns to look at me and hits my arm. "No way!"

I frown. "Sorry, it's just you ran off and didn't—"

"Not that! Look where we are."

BUT I FIND MYSELF

WE ARE SITTING beside a huge waterfall next to the trunk of the huge oak tree just outside of the city. I look down to see where the waterfall stops. It's the swirling ocean. The darkness is overtaking the water and climbing up toward us.

I try to act like everything is cool as I tell Caylee, "We should go."

She doesn't argue. We find our way to the brick road and try to blend in with the people, hoping no one will transform into a Trog. We are on the wrong side of the city in the center of the high-rise buildings. Caylee finds a pub and pulls me inside. We sit at a table in the corner and whisper.

"Do you remember where the bridge is?" Caylee asks.

"It's across the city by the carnival," I answer.

A plastic waitress walks up. "Drinks?"

I shake my head. Caylee glares at me. "Yes, thank you. We will have two mocha lattes."

"My favorite," I smirk. Just what I need, caffeine.

"I think we're in over our heads. We should call Mom and Dad," Caylee back-pedals.

She focuses all her energy and tries to call for them, when suddenly someone grabs her shoulder. "You have to help me."

We look up and see one of Caylee's friends from school, Sean.

Caylee looks horrified. "What are you doing here?"

"It's not what you think. Just come with me."

There's no time to ask questions. We follow him out of the café and around the corner. He takes us into an alley where there's one door. Ugh, a screen door. Sean goes in first. The room is full of people. Mothers are clinging to their children. Lovers are embracing. One small little girl is standing alone hugging her stuffed bunny.

"We have to get them out of here before it's too late." Sean is so morbid.

"Too late until?" Caylee asks.

"Until the darkness covers the city," he answers as if we're stupid.

"How long is that exactly?" I ask.

"Each hour the shadows approach and drag people away, screaming and begging for their life.

Once the darkness lifts, the partying begins again as if nothing happened." He turns to the window, his eyes darting up and down the street. He shuts the curtains and continues to explain, "We have to go quickly through the graveyard to the Wise-one. She's the only one who can lead us out of here." Sean points out of the window and through a dark field covered in headstones. Some are still standing, but none are in their original place. I see a shack on the hilltop with a dim light in the window.

"Okay, so what's the problem?" Caylee asks.

Sean points to the base of the hill. Huge dogs, rabid and foaming at the mouth, pace the out-skirts of the city. "No one is allowed out of this city, unless escorted by the shadows."

Caylee smiles one of her know-it-all smiles. "Well, it's a good thing I have a way with animals."

I drop my head to one side, "Oh really? I seem to remember a certain someone running from an animal not too long ago." Eyes narrowed, I skepti-cally raise an eyebrow. I'll believe it when I see it.

Caylee gives me a dirty look and acts like I didn't speak. She turns to Sean with a smile and asks. "How long before the shadows get here?"

"Seven minutes," Sean answers.

Shivers of excitement and dread cascade up my spine.

"I will go first and wave at you once it's safe," Caylee orders, "Then bring them out in groups of seven."

Caylee walks right out and approaches the growling dogs as if she has known them forever. They run at her with teeth showing. I start out the door to help, but Sean grabs my arm. I jerk my arm away and look back to find Caylee. Without explanation, the dogs pause and sit down. Caylee turns with a proud smile and waves her arms to motion for the first group.

I shake my head. This talent of hers would've been very useful earlier instead of running for our lives! Sean doesn't say a word to me. He opens the door and leaves with a group of seven. I start counting people off and sending them out the door every thirty seconds. No one argues. They just want out of here. Six minutes fly by, and there's only one group left.

Sean pushes inside. "We have to take cover before the shadows arrive. I'll go get Caylee."

He walks away. I stand there waiting for the real action to start.

The little girl with the bunny tugs on my shirt. "I'm scared. I want my mommy." Her bottom lip quivers. I look down on her.

What's a little kid doing in the kingdom of Darkness? I ask, "Where's your mom?"

The little girl points up.

I know she's not going to leave me alone. I look for a woman to coddle her, but there are only teenagers left. The little girl starts to cry. I roll my eyes and tap her shoulder, "Don't worry. Sean will take you to her."

Sean rushes in the door, pushing everyone toward the wall. "Take cover!"

"Where's Caylee?" I ask.

"No time. Get in the walls." He pushes me and the little girl behind a loose board.

The other five kids are shoulder to shoulder alongside us. I can smell the fear filling each one around me, flowing into my veins like a drug. I feel like I'm soaring above the room. The lights dim and shadows creep across the floor. A hissing darkness overtakes the cottage.

Screams from the city fill the air.

No one around me takes even a small breath while the darkness passes. Through a crack in the wall, I watch a shadow move by. Wearing the dark fog like a robe, I see a foot with black hair and long claws swing out from under its covering. Close behind the first shadow, another one floats by, combing the wall with its black nails.

I press my eye against the crack, hoping to see more. The shadow pauses in front of me. My eyes light up. I see its skeleton figure and gray skin clinging to its bones. Its face turns toward my peephole. I see its hollow skull searching for one to take. Each movement is swift and versatile. I want to reach out and feel his energy.

He steps in. I hold my ground until our eyes finally meet. I feel his loyalty and desire to serve me radiating from his strong eyes like when your guard dog crawls up in your lap and gazes at you begging for approval. He's ridding the kingdom of weakness—a necessary but thankless duty. I want to reach out.

A horrible, high-pitched sound fills the air, and the shadow quickly turns away, vanishing into light. Everyone around me gasps for air, but I drop my shoulders. I need more time. The little girl grabs my hand. Her energy flows into me, pure and innocent. It pulls me away from the fog, clearing my mind. I climb out of the wall and lead her over to Sean. He takes her hand and I move to the window to see if Caylee or anyone else is still out there.

The city lights pump back up and the party-ing picks right up where it left off. Noone appears shaken by the shadows' rampage. People are shoulder to shoulder in party mode strolling along the sidewalks, blocking my view through the window. I step out on the porch to look for Caylee, hoping she's nearby. People are everywhere. The dogs are still pacing at the bottom of the hill, but there's no sign of Caylee. Sean comes out of the cottage with the final group.

He asks me, "Do you see her?"

"No." My head involuntarily drops.

Sean goes into action. "Okay, let's get the last of these people to the Wise-one and then we'll worry about Caylee."

Everyone in the group forces a brave face and leaves the cottage. The dogs don't seem to care as we walk past them. I motion for the group to move on and head for the shack as I scan the horizon, hoping to see Caylee or more of the citizens of Dunabi. As soon as we step on the small porch, the door opens.

A little old lady scurries us inside. "Quickly, come in. Come in," she welcomes us as if we are visiting for tea.

We enter the small front room. There's a table set up with a marble game in front of a glowing fireplace.

The little round lady giggles. "Go, go, do not be afraid," she points to the fire.

The tall, skinny, blond kid runs straight into the fire and disappears. All the others follow without asking any questions. I'm standing there, staring as they shuffle into the flames and disintegrate. The little girl hugs me and says, "Thank you." She turns and skips into the fire. Why did she thank me?

The sweet little lady motions for me to sit across from her at the table. "Join me, won't you?"

I smile. How am I supposed to refuse such an old woman? I sit down and look at the game in front of me. There are lines of marbles for each player. The game is a marble race around the board and into your home. The problem: other players can kill you.

The lady rolls her dice and giggles. "A six! I'm out." Her nails clink against the board. She rolls again. "So, tell me, why you are here, Prince?"

I look up from the game. "I came to find my parents."

"Did you succeed?" She smiles and peers into my eyes.

"I found more than I planned on." I look down and pick up the dice.

She giggles in a high pitch. "Isn't that every-one's story down here?" She throws her head back, still giggling.

I roll the dice. Six. I'm out.

The lady rolls and taps her marble on the board as she moves it in my direction. "This world makes you believe that you have it all when really, you are the captive." She knocks my marble off the board. "Nothing is at it appears."

I catch my marble and look up to see her eyes flash into orange and red flames with an upright sliver of black for the cornea. In less than a second, her eyes return to normal. I tilt my head. She smiles, revealing large teeth discolored from the smoke seeping out of her throat. I look down and try to put my marble back on the board, hoping this sweet little lady doesn't turn me into a pile of ash.

Then she snaps, "You have a choice to make. Do not think as a child, decide as the prince who will prevail."

The front door bursts open. Caylee falls inside and slams it shut. Her hair looks like she ran through a forest and brought back a few limbs and a bird's nest. She turns to me and scrunches her face. "Of course you're playing a game while I am fighting those, those—"

The old lady finishes her sentence, "Troglodytes, honey. They have a name, just like you and I do. They also have a job to do, as do I." She stands and moves over to the fireplace.

Caylee doesn't smile and looks at me, pointing and mouthing silently, "Who is this?"

The lady giggles. "I am your portal home, dear."

Caylee's eyebrows rise. She instantly changes her attitude and smiles at the Wise-one. "Thank you." Caylee dips her head and tries to run her fingers through her hair, but a rat's nest stops her midway.

I chuckle, making Caylee's attitude change again. Not a happy girl.

Sean walks in the front door. Caylee tries to smooth her hair and smiles at him. I roll my eyes. Where did he go?

The old lady tilts her head. "Well, then, it's time to get you two moving." She twists her neck and coughs. Fire flows from her mouth and ignites the wood. "Step right up."

Caylee and I exchange slightly freaking out glances.

Sean grabs Caylee up in a hug. "Be strong and do not trust anyone." He shoots a quick look at me on the word *anyone*. He's standing in the same room as a dragon lady, but he doesn't trust me? Freak. A spark of anger lights inside of my chest. It's time to go. They hug a little too long. I'm not waiting, I jump into the flames.

READY TO FIGHT

SWIMMING THROUGH THE Wise-one's flames is nothing like swimming through water. It's hot and *HOT*. Not to mention, you can't see, at all! My hands finally hit cool air. I'm passing through the portal, I think. I bet I look like a puppy being held over water with his legs still swimming even though he's not in the water anymore. I pass through and fall over a sink, onto the floor beside a toilet, not very graceful for my first landing. The room is dark, but there's no mistaking the smell of a bathroom.

Just as I stand up to turn on the light, Caylee jumps through the mirror and hops off of the countertop, landing right on my back. I hit the ground, again. My face is not enjoying such close proximity to the bathroom floor.

Caylee scrambles to get off of me and grabs my arm, pulling me to my feet. She reaches over my shoulder and flicks on the light. Her face is completely red. I look around the room and recognize the towel on the rack. Home sweet home.

Caylee starts dusting me off, sweeping her hands all over my chest. "I am so sorry. Usually, I have better control. You know Canyon is the clumsy one. I am so sorry."

I grab her hands. "Caylee, it's all good." We're still holding hands. Awkward. I let go and turn away. "How did we end up here?"

She nods toward the mirror. "They've opened the mirrors as portals."

I smile. "Smart move."

She scowls and hits me, hard. "It's not smart! Johnny, they're following us!" She cocks her head sideways. "Or maybe they're following you."

We hear a scream of an inhuman kind followed by a freaking out human.

Caylee sticks her finger in my chest and orders, "Don't move."

She disappears out of the bathroom without opening a door or giving me a choice. I know I don't have to, but I respect Caylee's demand and stay in the bathroom, for now. I look into the mirror, trying to see any movement behind my reflection. Minutes pass, and I see nothing. They aren't following me.

I turn around and lean on the sink. The house is silent, too silent. I tap my fingers on the counter. What if Caylee needs my help? My patience is gone. I can't wait any longer. I exit the bathroom like a human through the door.

Darkness fills the hallway in an unnatural way. I hear whispers coming from my bedroom. I move along the wall and creep down the hall, listening.

"Look! This *thing* followed him through the portal," I recognize Canyon's voice.

Caylee says, "It's one of those nasty hunchbacks."

"No kidding. Of course I know what it is! I'm the one it attacked in the name of his prince!" Canyon's voice gets louder and then soft again.

Caylee argues, "Johnny's time is not up yet, he has *not* chosen."

"Oh really, well it looks to me like he *has!*"

Caylee lowers her voice to an angry whisper. "So! Either way, I'm with him."

Canyon huffs, "Me too, but you know what happens next if he goes dark."

"Yeah, the war will erupt and darkness will have the prevailing prince on their side," Caylee snaps back.

Then I hear Danielle whisper, "Either way, we need to be ready to fight."

I'm now standing in the doorway. I speak loudly, "You're right. So we need a plan."

All three sets of wide eyes jerk and turn in my direction. Busted.

Canyon blurts out, "How long you been standin' there, bro?"

I lower my brow. "Long enough, *bro*."

Danielle looks me up and down. "I like the new look."

I wink.

She blushes and Canyon laughs out loud.

Something crashes behind me. I cut my eyes down the hall and see a small creature scamper out of the bathroom. I look at Caylee, "Did you see that?"

Her facial expression answers before she says, "What?"

I look back down the hall into the darkness. It looks completely normal. Time to change the subject. "Nothing. So where is everybody?"

Canyon answers, "Mom left a note that the hospital called."

My mom! Without saying a word, I summon a portal and transport through the light to the hospital. All three follow right behind me. We pop into an empty hallway and start walking.

Canyon taps my shoulder. "Hey, we'll be in the waiting room down the hall. If you need us, just holler." He smiles as if something is wrong.

Caylee adds, "Mom and Dad are in there with Ms. Sara."

I nod and stare down the hall.

They all pass by and give me the same look as if we're at a funeral and I'm the one who just lost someone. I take a deep breath and make my way to see for myself how my mom really is. The white hallway seems forever long. I push open an unusually heavy door and enter her room.

Mom's feet are perfectly still under the sheet, nothing has changed. I fall into the chair next to her and put my head down on her arm, trying to understand what really happened underground. I saw her disappear.

A few moments pass. Mom's arm jolts and she grabs the bed rail. I jump up. She pulls up, gasping for air. Alarms sound from every machine. My mom turns, her wide eyes staring into mine. She lets out a deep sigh and starts pulling tape off of her mouth that's attached to her breathing tube. Nurses rush in front of me, trying to calm her down as they remove tubes and other life supports. Mom's reaching for me. A blond nurse gently pulls my arm and leads me to my mom's side as they continue to work on her.

As soon as her arms are free, Mom pulls me in close, and whispers in a hoarse voice, "I knew you would save me."

Mom's pulse rate increases. The head nurse enters the hospital room with a look of eviction on her face. I dart my eyes to Mom. She looks into my eyes. "I'm okay, sweetheart."

An elderly doctor charges in with a portable machine demanding I leave the room. The nurse sticks circular white pads all over my mom and attaches a bunch of wires.

I haven't moved. The doctor raises his voice, "You need to go to the waiting room, now."

I look back at Mom. She nods with a smile. After kissing her on the cheek, I walk to the door and pull the handle. Something doesn't feel right. I turn to look back one more time. The doctor and nurse are taking care of her. I'm sure she'll be okay.

I drag myself down the hall to find the waiting room. Ray, Susan, and Ms. Sara are sitting in a row of rigid blue chairs by the wall whispering intently to each other. Danielle, Caylee, and Canyon are sitting in front of the television arguing over what show to watch. I walk into the room, and all eyes turn to me.

My muscles are shaking. "She's awake." A slow smile forms. I have to fight back tears.

Susan stands. "Did she say anything?"

My lip quivers. "That she knew I would save her."

Canyon is staring, "And…"

"And then a doctor came in and wanted to do tests on Mom," I answer.

"Why did you have to leave?" Caylee asks as she offers me a blue Gatorade.

"He made me," I reply and take a drink of the cool blue liquid as I sit down next to Canyon.

Caylee's face twists. "That's weird. When Vanity was in the hospital after falling out of—"

I interrupt her with a shush and hold my Gatorade up. "Did you hear that?"

They all sit up tall and listen closely. Canyon grunts as he rattles the wrapper to his Twix. "Nah, I can't hear nothing but this stupid talk show Caylee had to watch. Why do we care about a priest interviewing girls who put suggestive pictures on their Facebook page?"

"Shhh, listen." I stand up, set the Gatorade down, and look out the doorway into the hall.

Ray is instantly beside me. "What's wrong?"

"I need to go to my mom." I attempt to walk out of the waiting room, but a hand on my right shoulder prevents my advancement.

To my left, Susan appears and tries to comfort me while Ray's big hand holds me in place. "She is fine. The doctors are great here and will take care of her. Come sit down for a minute and we'll ask the nurse how she is."

I hear the sound grow louder. I know it's my mom. Twisting out of Ray's hold, I rush out of the room and shout back, "My mom's screaming!"

I hear Ray tell Caylee, Canyon, and Danielle to stay in the waiting room. I know the adults are close behind me as I charge into my mom's hospital room.

It's empty.

The machines are pushed over. Her room looks worse than my closet. I turn, look at Ray, and immediately run out of the room to follow her fading screams to the elevators. The doors close and shut her screams inside. I hit the wall. This cannot happen! Everyone stands silently around me. Why do I always have to be the strong one? What if I'm tired of being strong? The elevator dings. I look up to see the numbers going down. Somehow, I know exactly where to go. I run down the stairs to the ground floor and through a set of double doors in the emergency room with a sign that reads, "Triage Room 3."

I burst inside the room and stop. I cannot believe what my eyes are seeing.

My chest rises and falls in extreme slow motion. I can feel the heat from the huge white lights shining in the center of the room. The doctor is perched on the side of a gurney, leaning over my mom. My heartbeat thrashes in my ears. The doctor is no longer feeble, but mighty, acting like a bloodthirsty vampire going in for the kill. Inhumanly, he twists his disfigured head to look at me with deep red eyes. I slowly inhale, breathing in a thick wall of sulfur. His skin drips off of his bones, exposing the tissue of his rock-hard muscles. My muscles tense as he leaps off of the gurney like a mountain lion and charges at me.

Before I can react, Ray has transformed into his Celestial form and is rolling on the floor, fighting the doctor. Ms. Sara is beside my mom, removing her restraints as Susan rummages through the cabinets, searching desperately for something.

In my mind, I hear Susan order, *Johnny, help me find a glass container!* Susan opens every door to every cabinet.

I help her dig through drawers as Ray throws the doctor across the room. The disfigured man hits the counter and violently rolls to the floor. His body shakes as if having a seizure.

Ray yells, "Now, Susan!"

"Johnny, I need *that* glass jar!" She points under the sink.

I see it. As I reach down, all sound in the room behind me ceases. I turn around to see a black fog rising from the disfigured doctor's mouth as his body arches into an extreme backbend. The fog swirls under the double doors and leaves. The disfigured doctor's body stops seizing and puddles on the floor. His huge size and inhuman features regress back into the human form of the elderly doctor. Ms. Sara frees my mom as Ray tends to the doctor.

"He has a weak pulse. We must find the demon before it enters another host body," Ray orders.

Susan asks Ms. Sara, "Will you take Johnny and Maranda back to her hospital room?"

"Of course, you and Ray go catch that thing," Ms. Sara blurts.

Ray and Susan nod and charge toward the double doors, but the doors swing open toward them before they get out. A large, dark figure enters the room. They're ready for battle when a familiar voice echoes, "What's going on in here?" Canyon's standing before us finishing his Twix. Relief fills the room, until we see his eyes. They're a deep red.

SHADOWS APPROACH

RAY ADVANCES TOWARD Canyon. "Son, where have you been?"

Canyon laughs and sarcastically answers, "In the waiting room upstairs, Dad. Remember, that's where you left us? What's going on in here?" He pops the last bite of chocolate into his mouth.

Caylee and Danielle burst in behind Canyon. Caylee tries to explain their intrusion. "Sorry, but Canyon was getting mad at an old lady who started smoking in the waiting room because it was making his eyes burn. So we came downstairs to get fresh air and another snack." She rolls her eyes and points at Canyon. He shrugs his shoulders and keeps chewing. Caylee continues, "Then we heard Mom ask for a glass container and, well, we all know what that means. We couldn't just sit back while y'all were in danger. So, here we are." Caylee holds up a glass bottle with half of her drink in it as a peace offering.

Canyon says the obvious, "Glass jar," then he bows his chest out and yips, "Check!"

Susan smiles at Caylee and takes the glass. "I wonder if demons can swim?" She tilts her head at Canyon as she walks behind him. Canyon looks over his shoulder. Susan pops open the jar, ready to test her hypothesis.

Caylee looks at her mom like she's crazy.

Ray puts his hand on Canyon's arm. "Canyon, we need you to switch to spiritual time."

Canyon blurts out, "Okay, but why are y'all acting so weird? You act like it is against the law to eat a Twix." Instantly, the clock is frozen, and we're all in the spirit. Canyon is still Canyon. No demon.

Susan switches us back to carnal time. Ray immediately asks, "Caylee, what exactly did this woman look like?" She describes an elderly woman with purplish-gray curly hair wearing a red hat and carrying a red purse. Ray and Susan charge out of the double doors and back upstairs with the glass jar.

Canyon grunts, "What's their problem?"

I walk over to my mom and grab her hand. "Mom, are you okay?"

She opens her eyes and nods with a sweet smile.

I lean over and kiss her forehead. "I'm glad you're back."

Mom whispers, "Me too," and lets go of my hand.

I look toward the door, wondering if Ray and Susan have found the demon yet. My mom reads my mind. "You can go. I'll still be here when you get back."

I tilt my head. "What?"

Mom smiles. "You're just like your father. Go on. Follow what's inside of you."

If you only knew. I shake my head.

I guess Mom thinks my silence equals panic. She tries to calm my steady nerves. "I'm sure they could use some more warriors to help finish this. Don't worry, Ms. Sara will stay with me."

I look at Ms. Sara. "Take care of her until I get back, okay?" Ms. Sara nods and helps my mom into a wheelchair. No more gurneys!

Caylee, Canyon, and Danielle are huddled by the door, whispering.

I creep up between the girls and yell, "Hey! Anyone want to go demon hunting?"

Danielle gasps for air and grabs her chest.

Caylee slugs me. "Don't sneak up on us like that. You wanna get hurt?"

"Aren't you my Guardian? Really?"

She laughs and Canyon steps up, "Never mind them, Johnny. I've got your back. Let's go." He opens the door for me and rolls his eyes at the girls. Caylee grabs Canyon by the collar and jerks him back out of her way. The pull gags Canyon. He tugs on his collar to get it off of his throat and stomps out of the room behind the girls.

Ms. Sara hollers after us, "You kids play nice and stay together!"

We all laugh. Since when do teens play nice, ever? Caylee and Canyon race upstairs. Danielle and I win; we took the elevator.

Together, we walk into the waiting room on the second floor, the location of the last sighting of the old woman with the purple hat and red purse.

I look at the twins. "Okay, where was it?"

Canyon points at the restroom in the back corner of the waiting room. "It went in there."

With my shoulders high, I walk right up to the door and open it. The light is flickering. I should know the warning signs by now, but I step inside as if everything is normal. There's dirt around the drain in the sink.

I hear Caylee ask Canyon, "Where's Mom and Dad?"

Then something drops from the ceiling. When am I going to remember to check *up* before jumping in? I raise my eyes to see one of the tiles slightly out of place. A shadow crosses the tile, knocking another clump of dirt down into the sink.

I jump up on the countertop and lift the ceiling tile just enough to stick my head inside and look around. There's a lot of duct work and wires. Something moves right in front of me. I focus my eyes and see a large thing crawl across the ceiling like a rodent. Then a few more scamper behind it. Soon there's a row of glowing eyes staring back at me.

Caylee yells from below, "What's up there?"

I look down. "A lot of eyes."

Canyon's color fades. "Like how many eyes?"

"Too many."

Canyon moans. I've seen enough. I start to duck out, but someone in the ceiling whispers, "Worship the one who prevails." I straighten back up and look around one more time.

To my right is a creature with a large jaw and wide red eyes standing within two feet of my face. He raises his arm and yells, "The one who prevails!"

The swarming creatures crowd around and face me. They raise their arms and follow his chant, screaming, "The one who prevails!" I scan the ceiling, looking from creature to creature, realizing they're in awe of me. My face perks up. No longer am I creeping out. In fact, I feel quite the opposite. These are *my* creatures of the dark chanting out *my* praises.

Something grabs my leg and pulls me down into the bathroom. I can still hear the chanting from above. I look around the bathroom. Both twins and Danielle are holding their hands over their ears and squinting their eyes.

Canyon screams, "Can't you hear that?"

I don't know what to say.

Danielle begs as if her life depends on it, "Make it stop, please, make it stop!"

I pull myself back up into the ceiling tile and lift my hand. Silence falls across the black ceiling. Every red eye is on me, anticipating my words.

Before I can speak, a loud screech like someone's cutting glass fills the tiny bathroom below me. I jump off the sink and down to the floor as a large boot crosses through the mirror. Within seconds, a nine-foot man with pale skin and sharp features is standing beside the sink. He stares at us and we stare back. No one moves.

Another foot crosses. This one is not as large but leads to a tall, skinny guy with red crazy hair and even more crazy eyes. Like a robot, he steps next to the other guy and stands in line, staring at us. The ends of my nerves feel like an electrical charge just hit them. These two are disgustingly amazing.

Caylee speaks into my mind, *What now?*

Canyon answers, *We fight.*

I jerk my head and glare at Canyon, *No, let me find out what they want.* I look at the first guy and ask, "What's your purpose here?"

He drops his eyes and kneels. The other guy follows his lead.

I look at the twins and shrug my shoulders. The Hollow Man speaks inside of me, *They're here to serve you.*

My heart seems to freeze, but then pounds in my chest. *I don't need their service.*

Oh, but you do. The Hollow Man laughs at me.

Why?

There's a lot more coming, the Hollow Man warns.

A lot more what?

The Hollow Man is silent.

I yell out loud, "A lot more what!"

The twins and the guys are now staring at me. I look around and try to cover my insanity. "A lot more than kneeling is required. Stand and tell me what is coming."

Crazy Red Hair starts laughing a sick belly rolling laugh. He looks up at Danielle and smiles with yellow sharp teeth. Drool drips down his face.

The big guy rises and declares, "The Army of Darkness."

"Why?" I ask, forcing my voice to remain steady.

"We have been sent to serve the Prince of Darkness."

"I have *not* chosen a kingdom! I'm the prince of nothing."

The Crazy Red Hair's voice dances as he fidgets, "You are our prince, the one who will prevail."

I want to cut off his head. "What makes you think I'm over the darkness?"

The big guy looks right in my eye. "The Queen has spoken."

I shift back on my heels. There is only one way around this. "Take me to the Queen!"

Danielle grabs my arm. "Johnny, no!"

In a flash, the two men attack. Crazy Red Hair slides up behind Danielle and wraps his arms around her, pulling her off her feet. She yelps. The look on her face burns into my memory. I move forward as the redhead smells the side of her face and licks her with his rotten tongue. I pull a sword from nowhere and use pure instinct as I swing.

The big guy catches my blade. "Prince, you are either for us or against us."

I lower my sword. How am I supposed to choose?

The Hollow Man whispers, *You know where you belong.*

Caylee is already on the redhead and swinging him across the small bathroom into the tile wall. Danielle runs out of the bathroom, wiping her face a hundred miles an hour. Canyon and the big guy are now squaring up. I look out into the waiting room and see the same red-eyed creatures dropping out of the ceiling and crowding around Danielle. She jumps on top of two chairs, kicking them as if she's at soccer practice, but there are too many. Three find their way up her back scaling her like a rock climber as their blades dig into her flesh. Danielle's shoulders cave in, her face crumples. She's fading.

The Hollow Man tells me, *You know how to handle this. Take authority already.*

I can and I will. My back straightens up. I feel the anger crawling inside of me; I focus and let the energy pulsate through my mind.

I let go.

The light flashes and knocks the beasts to the ground. They won't be down for long. I've got to get Danielle out of here. I run over and grab her hand. She jumps off of the chairs. One of the beasts grabs her ankle and digs it claws into her flesh. Danielle reaches down to knock him off, but two more creatures jump on her back. I've had enough.

"Stop!" My voice echoes through the waiting room.

The creatures on Danielle stop in place and drop their jaws. It's as if they just now noticed me in the room. The one around her ankle crawls off slowly, hoping I don't see him. I motion for Danielle to move toward the door. She flicks the two creatures off her back as if they were tiny insects annoying her. I step toward the door and notice the creatures following me. I stop and turn to face the crowd. "Stay!" I point at them like I would a dog. Step by step, I back out of the waiting room and spill into the empty hallway, making sure the door shuts behind us. My lungs are transferring oxygen to my cells as fast as possible. Danielle's completely freaking out.

She gasps. "How did you do that!"

I shrug.

She slugs my arm. "Don't act innocent. How did you control those…those things?" Her breathing escalates to the point I'm concerned she will hyperventilate at any moment.

I stop and grab her shoulders so that she's looking right at me. "Danielle, I need you to go tell Ms. Sara what you just saw. I have to help Caylee and Canyon." A calm voice from behind me says, "Looks like I arrived at just the right time."

I turn to see Shay standing there with a bouquet of flowers. I smile and let go of Danielle's shoulders. I don't know how to respond to this girl. Fear and infatuation struggle for the lead.

Shay picks up on my inability to respond. "I came to visit your mom. I can't believe she's awake."

I tip my head. "How did you know where and who my mom was?" I want to ask her for the real reason she decided to *visit* my mom, but I know that would open a can of worms that I don't really have time for right now.

"It's all over town, Johnny. Everyone knows."

I've got to get my mom out of here. If Shay knows where she is, then the entire dark kingdom knows.

Danielle's eyes plead with me to stay with her.

I look at Shay, "Danielle can take you to my mom's room, 216. I'll be right there." I turn to Danielle. She glares at me with an angry smile.

I pat her arm and say, "Ms. Sara is expecting you. Tell her it's time to go."

Shay smiles and dips her head as if she's a nice little girl with manners. "Sounds like a plan. She grabs Danielle's arm. Danielle flinches. "Oh come on, I won't bite." Shay laughs and looks over her shoulder at me, flashing her inhuman eyes. "Don't worry, I've got this under control."

That's exactly what I'm worried about.

I watch them walk down the hall, arm in uncomfortable arm, toward my mom's hospital room.

No time to worry. I have to help the twins. I turn my head and concentrate on the waiting room. An army of hairy hunchbacks steps out of the waiting room and stares me down. I square up, ready to fight. The lead guy speaks to the group with an authoritative tone in a language unfamiliar to me.

The group snaps their feet together in unison and then salutes me. A few seconds pass, they stand at ease and turn to march the other way.

Three nurses are walking straight into the crowd of hunchbacks. This is not going to be good. I brace for hysteria, but the nurses don't even bat an eye. Instead they all smile and move over to the other side of the hallway to make way for the group. The hunchbacks nod at the women and disappear around the corner.

Then I hear the tall blond nurse say, "The guy in the back with black hair was adorable! I wonder if he's single?"

The shorter nurse laughs. "You should run back and make an excuse to talk to him. I'm sure they stopped at the nurse's station."

The blond shuffles past me. "No, I don't want to make a fool of myself. You know how I melt for a guy in uniform."

They walk off giggling. I shake my head. There's no time to worry about the sanity of nurses, I need to get back to the twins. The waiting room is crawling with tiny creatures worse than a roach infestation. There's only one way in and one way out—through the mass. I straighten up and step into the large room.

The TV is still playing a talk show. A few of the beasts notice me and move out of my way. With each step, more of them back up to open a path for me to pass through. No claws, no teeth, just humble servants.

I walk right up to the bathroom door and open it expecting to find Caylee and Canyon, but it's completely empty. I look up before stepping inside. The tiles are in place. Everything is sparkling white. I spin around. Where could they have gone? There's no way out unless they went...

I stand on the toilet and reach up. The tile moves easily allowing me to stick my head through the opening and look around. Tiny beasts are scurrying all around. There's no longer a few.

I put the ceiling tile back and hop down. I have to find Caylee and Canyon. I rush through the waiting room. The beasts move up and down the rows of chairs, climbing the walls and chattering to each other. There's no method to their madness. I walk out of the waiting room into the empty hallway and take a deep breath.

I put my hands on the sides of my face. Think, Johnny, think. Where would the twins go? I feel a sudden presence approach. I drop my hands and turn to see Susan and Ray with three other warriors. They are huge!

Susan asks the question of the day, "Where are Caylee and Canyon? And why aren't they with you?"

I Have To Find Them

"THEY WERE IN the bathroom, fighting, protecting me. I left them to help Danielle fight a hundred more Trogs in the waiting room." I drop my head, "When I went back, they were gone."

Ray demands, "Show me where you last saw them."

I start to walk and then turn back. "It won't be easy getting through all of the beasts. Just follow me."

One of the new guys laughs. "Don't worry about us, we've been doing this for a while."

I walk into the waiting room. It's completely empty. I feel every liter of my blood drop to my feet. What's going on? My eyes dart to the Johnsons.

The two big guys in the back are swapping sarcastic expressions.

Susan refocuses me. "Go on, Johnny. Where were they?"

I force my feet to lead us to the bathroom and I open the door.

Caylee pushes Canyon. "I told you he would come back!"

Canyon blurts, "Well, it took him long enough!" He turns to me, "Why did you leave us in here so long? It's kind of weird to be locked in a bathroom with your sister."

Ray glares, "And please explain to me why you didn't transport out?"

Canyon shrugs his shoulders.

Caylee defends, "We tried, but something held us in here."

Everyone looks at me.

"What?"

The Hollow Man jeers, *Of course this is all your fault.*

I look up when the shortest seven-foot warrior of the group asks, "Okay, where are all of these beasts?"

My face is getting hot. "They were in there." I point to the waiting room.

The adults look around and then look back at me with tight faces and narrow eyes.

Ray rubs the back of his neck, "Well, they're gone now."

Canyon tries to help, "Danielle is the one who screamed. Where's she at?"

Susan's lips are pressed tight together. "She's in Maranda's room with Ms. Sara and Shay."

Ray lowers his hands and folds his arms, "What kind of games are you kids playing?"

I stare at my feet. There's no way to prove any of this.

The Hollow Man speaks at the most inopportune times. *They think you're a liar. Why would you want to live for eternity with people who are so quick to judge?*

I fold my arms. This is not how I thought things would play out.

Caylee intervenes, "There was something there, Dad. We heard them."

A flash of red eyes passes through my mind. I jump up on the sink and lift the ceiling tile. With a smirk, I motion for Ray, "See for yourself."

Ray moves into the bathroom and doesn't even have to stretch to reach the ceiling tile, "Okay, but this is the last—" He stops talking and lowers the tile back into place. He motions for everyone to step out of the bathroom.

Susan is the first to ask, "What?"

Ray's in warrior mode. "We have a portal."

"How many of them are there?" Susan asks.

"Too many." Ray's eyes are small.

Hey, that's what I said!

The tall guy asks, "What's the assignment?"

Ray responds, "Destroy the portal."

Two of the men walk into the bathroom and shut the door.

Canyon elbows Caylee and laughs. "And I thought it was weird for you and I to be in there alone."

She rolls her eyes. "You're so immature."

"What?" Canyon's voice cracks.

Susan takes over. "Ray, what are we going to do about the ones who have already stepped over?"

"We fight." His voice seems to rattle the beasts overhead. We hear a large amount of movement causing debris to fall all around us. Ray and Susan move into their fighting stances, back to back, supernatural warriors.

Susan looks at Canyon. "We will hold them off here. You three go stop the demon inside the old woman, she must be the one opening the portals."

The tile drops and a flood of beasts fill the room. Caylee grabs my arm and pulls me toward the door. Susan is completely covered by creatures, biting and stabbing her. A strong heat consumes me, pulling me back inside the room. I want to help Susan, but

I'm not sure who needs my help more, Susan or the creatures.

Ray spins and projects a light that slices through one section of beasts, cutting them in half, spewing their dark red blood across the room. He flashes into a light and surrounds Susan. A burst of energy comes from Ray that sounds like a light bulb popping. Beasts roll across the room, jump up, and charge after the Johnsons again. Susan's bleeding from her wounds, but she doesn't stop fighting. With her sword raised, she's ready for more.

Canyon yells at me, "There's no time for bystanders. Either you're in this or not!"

He turns and I follow him, running down the hall and around the corner.

The nurse's station is completely abandoned. The elevators are straight ahead. Canyon's eyes dart all around as he checks every corner for any sign of life.

"Where did everyone go?" Canyon asks.

I laugh. "Oh, they're still here."

He jerks his head to look at me. The elevators ring and we hear the doors open. Caylee and Canyon duck behind the nurse's desk. Canyon pulls me down to hide with them. I roll my eyes and follow along as if I need to hide from those who serve me.

A familiar group of footsteps exits the elevator and stomps in unison as they pass in front of the desks. We hear them turn the corner and fade into the distance. Canyon leans over to get a look.

"There are six nasty looking hunchbacks." He shivers. "And you wonder why I hate the dark."

Caylee shushes him and points behind us. I hear labored breathing with a soft whimper come from behind the filing cabinet. Caylee crawls over and peeks. She jumps up and kneels over something behind the cabinet. A few seconds later, she turns around, slowly shaking her head.

Canyon asks, "What?"

She crawls over to him and sits down, "You don't want to know."

Canyon huffs, "Right, like it's sooooo scary hiding behind a filing cabinet."

She leads the way with her arm. "Suit yourself."

Canyon raises his chin and passes by us on all fours. He crawls to the edge and turns his head. Every ounce of blood runs out of his face. He slumps back. "Why did you let me look?"

Caylee slugs his arm. "Suck it up. A little blood never hurt anyone. We need to find whatever did that to her."

I follow my new first instinct and look up. The tiles are all in place. I scan around the perimeter of the room. Then I see only one hospital room door open. I put my finger to my lips and motion for them to follow me, but they're too busy discussing how it's impossible for the blood-covered nurse to still be moaning when she's dead. Neither of them notice when I slip around the desk and stand. No point in crawling.

Grunting and smacking sounds charge out of the open hospital room. I have a little too much confidence and walk right up to the door. A five-foot guy, bone thin with white ash skin, is leaning over the hospital bed, devouring the human and his soul. He turns to me with blood dripping down his chin. I stare, expecting repulsion to make me run away, but nothing happens. Instead, I stare. He puts down his food and steps toward me. His bony knees look too weak to hold his frame up, but his stride is that of an athlete. In one swift movement, he is at my feet, bowing. I want to reach out and bestow my approval, but something is holding me back. A growing sensation of disgust is trying to dominate. I step back.

A gust swarms from behind me. Canyon. He tackles the man and grabs him around his neck. The man is flailing and screeching at Canyon. I want to help, but I want Canyon to let him go. Canyon rolls on top of the creature and gains leverage. He's about to snap his neck. I charge toward Canyon and push him over. The creature jumps to his feet and leaps on top of Canyon. He places his hands around Canyon's neck. The ends of his fingers extend the bones and dig into Canyon's flesh. Canyon opens his mouth and screams as a swarm of maggots crawl out and down his face.

Anger convulses through me.

I let go.

A flash of light pulses through the room and knocks the creature to the floor, motionless. Canyon rolls to his side, gasping for air and spitting. I feel a presence behind me. Caylee's standing there with her hands on her hips, smiling. How long has she been there?

I want to rush to Canyon's side, but my body will not move.

The Hollow Man laughs. *So you want to prolong his suffering. Nice move. Demented. But nice move.*

Caylee pats me on the back and kneels down beside Canyon. She helps him up to his knees. His chest is heaving. He stops and falls over on all fours. His stomach convulses followed by a flow of maggot-filled vomit. Canyon spits and raises his chin to send a clear message to me.

Caylee is next to him looking at me, but not with anger. Respect.

Something crashes in the hallway. I run. Caylee and Canyon are right behind me. We slide around the corner just in time to see a red purse disappear into an elevator. We stop and watch the numbers light up. The old lady's elevator stops at the second floor, my mom's floor. I push the button to the elevator. Time is moving so slow. I can feel Canyon's vision searing into my back. I tap my leg and try to remain focused.

He cannot hold back. "What just happened back there, Johnny?"

I push the button ten more times as if it will arrive any faster. "I saved your ass. That's what happened."

"Before you saved me…"

My fingers tap faster. "It was so fast. I just did what I had to do."

"So, you had to almost kill me before you saved me?"

I twist around. "I would never kill you, Canyon!" The elevator dings and opens. All three of us walk inside the little box, silently. Canyon's face increases in color with each second that passes.

He's almost lobster red when he bursts out, "At least explain why that thing was bowing to you."

I stare at him.

The Hollow Man tells me, *Go ahead, Prince; tell him what he wants to hear.*

The elevator door opens at the perfect moment. I sidestep around Canyon to face a bigger problem. The old woman is right in front of me, but she's not alone. She has Danielle sitting behind the receptionist desk posed as if she's an employee of the hospital. There are tons of bony people, staring and drooling as if something is physically holding them back from their human dinner. Where's Mom? I look around the room, but she's not here. Danielle and I meet eyes. She's terrified.

Caylee and Canyon are on each side of me. I feel like we're the law standing on a dirt street in an old western movie facing off with the bad guys. The old woman moves behind Danielle and places her purse on the counter. Then she scrapes her hands across Danielle's shoulder. I watch as the skin on the woman drops to the floor like an untied hospital gown. She's nothing but bones with stringy grey hair and a purple hat on top. The old woman arches her fingers over Danielle's head and laughs as she slams her hands down and jabs her nails into Danielle's shoulders. Danielle screams from the pain. The old woman's bones start to enter Danielle's body, taking possession of her. Time to move.

I run straight ahead. Caylee takes the left. Canyon's on my right. They jump into immediate hand-to-bone combat. I take on the old lady. With no effort, I leap over the counter and knock her backward off of Danielle. I hear the old woman's chest bones break as she hits the tile floor. Danielle is released from the old woman's power and gasps for air.

Caylee spins around and sweep kicks a dozen bony people, knocking them to the ground. Another line of skeletons step over the ones on the floor and charge at her. She doesn't seem to be phased and continues to fight.

Canyon is crashing skulls together and throwing them into a pile. No worries, there are only a couple hundred more to take down.

I untie Danielle. "You need to get out of here." Danielle wraps her arms around me. I hug her tightly and whisper, "I will come for you. Find an empty room and lock the door." Danielle smiles and lets go of me. I watch her run down the hall checking rooms until she disappears into the last one on the left.

I turn and prepare to fight.

Time Runs Out

I STAND THERE for minutes, watching Caylee and Canyon fight hundreds of skinless beasts. Not one approaches me. They all go after the twins. I step forward and look into their faces. A red glow passes from one to another, but disappears when they're dismembered by the twins. I look down at the growing piles. My chest aches. I want to breathe life back into the bones.

The Hollow Man makes the ache in my chest increase. *How can you watch your people be slaughtered? They're here to serve you!*

Involuntarily, I step toward Canyon's pile of bones. I feel like I'm having an out of body experience, watching myself kneel at the pile and reach out to touch the bones. I close my eyes and focus all of my emotion.

I let go.

A strong wind encircles me. I open my eyes and see a red glow in the center of bones, enlarging to completely swallow up the bones. I stand and back out of the wind, watching the power pick up every bone. As they fly within the funnel, the bones reconnect. They're coming back to life!

The ceiling trembles. I look up. The tile between Canyon and me falls to the floor. My eyes meet Canyon's. He moves toward me. Enraged.

The Hollow Man antagonizes me, *Look how quickly the light turns on its own. Is this the kind of people you want to serve? They act so perfect yet they are so full of lies.*

I stand my ground and look into Canyon's angry eyes as he charges toward me. I'm ready to rock and roll.

The lights flicker. Caylee is yelling at Canyon to stop. I don't want to kill him. Suddenly an infestation of the small beasts floods down like a waterfall from the open tile separating me from Canyon. Then my ears are filled with a scream from a hospital room behind me. I turn and run to find Danielle.

Door to door, I kick them open. The sounds of battle tempt me to turn around, but the desperate scream in front of me pulls me on. Footsteps bang on the tiles above my head. I keep going. Every door swings open with a swift kick. The patients are either still in their beds, frozen, or missing. The rooms of the missing are in complete disarray and covered in blood, pushing me harder to find Danielle.

I'm near the end of the hall. The scream is close. I know this is the room, and I kick with all of my might. The door fights back and slams me against the wall across the hall. The impact forces my lungs to empty. I stand up and take a deep breath before I run and jump at the door again as if I'm a ninja with superpowers. The door opens too easily and I fly eight feet into the room, sliding across the floor and hitting the bottom of the bed. I jump to my feet just as the door slams shut.

The room is dark. My eyes are adjusting, I can almost see. A high-pitched scream pulsates through the room. I think I'm prepared to fight anything until I hear a voice whisper from behind me, "I knew you would come to rescue me."

I stand still as she moves in front of me. I feel her face near mine. "My hero." Her lips press into mine. Shay. I crumble under her trance.

Her hands move to my chest. "You are so amazing."

"Really? Why's that?"

She drags her fingers through my hair. I force my eyes to stay open. "Because, here you are fighting for the ones you love and fighting against the ones who serve you. When are you going to realize that you can have both?"

My head tilts. "How so?"

"You are the prince. Your people must obey your command. Just say the word, Johnny."

Manipulation is powerful. I am powerful.

Shay places her soft hand on my face. "Whatever *you* allow will continue." She moves her lips back onto mine. This, I am allowing!

Her hands glide down my neck and scour my body until she finds her way under my shirt and pulls me toward her.

A loud crash outside our door reminds me where I am. My head feels like it is just now getting oxygen and thinking clearly. I pull away, Shay tries to stop me.

I push past her. "Shay, I can't stay here and hide. This is my battle."

I shove the door open and run back to the twins.

I hear Shay's heels clicking behind me as she yells down the hall, "Johnny, what exactly are you fighting for?"

As soon as I reach the nurse's station, I try to find Caylee and Canyon. There are swarms of beasts filling every corner. Then I see a light flash. Canyon. I run toward him. This is what I am fighting for.

The elevators ding. I turn to see Ray, Susan, and their entourage spill into the room. Fits gonna hit the shan.

The Hollow Man reminds me, *You're the prince. Why are you running into battle? Let the weak die and the strong reign.*

I pause.

Everything around me is escalating so fast. The room feels like it is moving all around me in complete chaos—war and fighting, death and dying. I want to help, but I'm hungry for more. My stomach, my soul, growls.

Shay walks up beside me and slips her hands around my waist. "Amazing, isn't it?"

This girl doesn't give up.

I turn to tell Shay to go. Over her shoulder, I see Danielle standing at the end of the hall. Danielle's head drops and she disappears back into the hospital room.

I dart my eyes to Shay. "What's so amazing?"

She points to the room. "Having such power."

My eyes follow her hand. More warriors enter the hospital with swords drawn. The battle is in full force. Piles of dead beasts collect in every corner like killing an infestation of disgusting insects. No one grieves. In fact, they're satisfied to rid the world of one more ugly thing. I stand there and watch the mayhem, unable to move.

Susan crosses my line of sight. Something's wrong. She forces her way through the fighting toward the twins. I don't see Canyon's light anymore. Caylee and Ray are taking out as many beasts as possible, trying to keep the Troglodytes back with swords slicing through the air. I pull away from Shay and move to help them. Susan kneels down over Canyon and starts shaking him. Each step I take increases in speed. I have to save him. Susan's body slumps and she stops moving Canyon. Her eyes meet mine. A mixture of grief and fury flow into my veins. No! I will not let this happen. Susan's eyes are overwhelmed with tears. She lifts her head and releases a wail from the depths of sorrow. The sound stops all forms of time and sends a quake throughout the entire floor. Beasts fall to their instant death. Celestials in the room fall to their knees. Caylee hits the floor. She's not moving, not breathing. Ray covers her, a bright light flashes, shattering every piece of glass in its path.

This. Cannot. Happen.

Nothing's Left

I GRAB MY head. No one has ever loved me like they love me. I stumble backward and hit the wall. They're the only family I've got left. My chest heaves into hyperventilation.

The Hollow Man speaks at the wrong time, *This is all for a reason. It's time for you to let the weak go.*

I scream, and not in my head, "No!" I push off the wall. A deep energy builds. Anger manifests inside of me, but this time, I'm in complete control.

I let go.

A surge of light bursts out of my body. The Hollow Man tumbles to the floor in front of me. The room feels empty, except for the Hollow Man and me. He rises with a flaming fury.

Fire versus light.

"You will not take my friend!"

He screams back at me, "Me? You are blaming me?" The Hollow Man walks up to my face. "Take a good look, Prince, I am you!"

I stare into his hollow eyes and see myself looking back. His height, build, hair length, everything is exactly the same as me. This can't be true. I'm not a killer.

He backs up. "You're not a killer, really? Think back, Johnny. You have killed plenty by simple words or actions. You think you're so innocent because you have not spilled blood, but you have spilled plenty of souls."

My entire body is lighting up. Flames consume the Hollow Man, heat radiating off him. Electricity flows through every one of my veins as I jump toward him. My energy pulses into the air molecules around us. The moment we impact each other, an electric field ignites around us, casting a violet light throughout the air as if a lightning storm has taken over the hospital. Our power surges through every bit of metal, violet streams of light dance throughout the room. I focus on my hollow eyes. The energy pulls us closer.

He whispers, "The darker the night, the brighter the day."

Flashes of violet surround us, consuming my power. My muscles weaken. The Hollow Man pushes me. I stumble into an orb of violet light.

With each step backward, I feel the air around me thickening. I hear water flowing and smell sulfur. I'm no longer in the hospital.

❧

To my left and right, there are lines of people standing along the edge of the river, staring into the rolling water as it disappears over the edge of the dark waterfall. Their eyes are dark, shoulders down, and arms seem to just hang next to them. Lifeless.

A lady next to me takes a large step forward and falls into the water. I reach out to catch her, but she's gone. I run alongside the river, looking for the woman in the water. As I search, I see many faces, hollow faces. They aren't struggling against the water. They are letting it take them over the edge.

I back up. Small children, adults, elderly couples each step off to their eternal demise. Willingly.

I rub my neck and pace up and down the edge of the water. My eyes cannot see enough of the faces floating away. There is no fight left in them. They are...weak. Disposed of. Forever.

It's time to find a way out of here. I walk upstream and pass hundreds of hopeless people. Then I see a familiar couple holding hands. Their eyes are different, sad. Not willing. I step closer. They turn to look at me. The moment

I see the woman's eyes, I know who they are. I run. I have to save them, not for me, but for Danielle.

The Hollow Man appears behind the woman. My legs amp up to full speed. I want to scream at him to stop, but my vocal cords refuse to work. The woman looks at me, begging me to save her. The man is grasping her hand, tears running down his face. I'm close.

The Hollow Man looks at me and throws his head back. His laughter rings in my ears. He places both hands on the woman's back. I try to scream, but the Hollow Man speaks for me, "You have made your choice."

He pushes. She falls into the water, releasing her husband's hand. Her husband refuses to let go. With every ounce of energy he tries to pull her back to shore. The Hollow Man stands behind him, laughing.

His laugh stops.

He glares at me. "Pathetic, really. There's no room in our world for weakness."

He lifts his foot and shoves the man over. The couple sinks below the water's surface.

No! Without a second thought, I jump in, swimming through water and bodies. I can see them a few feet from me, but the water is too powerful. I can feel the edge of the falls approaching as the water rips me back and forth. Hands and legs slap against me, forcing me further under.

I fall over the edge. Water is spraying across my face and punching me around like a ragdoll.

Falling.

No worries. No thoughts.

Falling.

My body slams into a brick wall of ocean waves. Lifeless people are all around me. No one is fighting. I close my eyes, I am not fighting. I feel the air around me thinning out. I see a violet light.

The Hollow Man won.

I won.

⁂

My eyes open. I'm back, standing in the middle of the battle at the hospital. Swords clang, beasts bleed, Celestials lose their light, and I watch.

I'm killing them.

The old woman with the red hat runs across the room and down the hall. I've got to stop the demon from opening any more portals. I follow behind her. She looks over her shoulder and laughs. I speed up. She stops in front of the door to room 216, my mom's room, and puts her hand to her throat, slicing her fingers across her neck. I hold the scream in the back of my throat and race to protect my mom. Without opening the door, the old woman passes through. I'm right on her heels.

She hovers over the person in the hospital bed. Mom.

I stop, hoping to bargain with the demon inside of the old woman. "What do you want?"

Her voice squeaks, "Why, Prince, you know exactly what I want." From within the old woman, the demon's voice growls, "Her soul."

Never will she take my mom's soul. I step toward the old woman ready to fight.

She places her hands around my mom's neck. My mom pulls at her fingers, gasping for air. I stop and focus my anger on the old woman.

The old woman tilts her head. "Why does the prince want to protect a traitor?"

My muscles twitch. "How dare you suggest my mother is a traitor!"

The old woman leans back, roaring in a demonic laughter. "Your mother? Do you seriously believe a human can produce a god?" She keeps one hand on my mom's neck, while flailing the other one in the air to exaggerate her laughter.

I drop my voice. "Take your hands off of my mom."

The old lady stops laughing and the demon growls, "She is not your mother!" She looks down at my mom, "Tell him the truth, Maranda."

I look at my mom. Tears stream down her face. "I have always loved you as my own."

I step back. What is my mom saying? I shake my head and refuse to listen.

The old woman taunts, "What's the matter, Prince? Have you lost your mommy?"

I look into my mom's eyes. They are brown. No way. I take another step back.

My mom begs, "Johnny, don't listen to her. I will explain it all to you when we have time. For now, I need you to trust me."

My body feels weak. She's the only mother I know. She's the one who has raised me and loved me. My head drops. I want to scream and I want to cry. Sudden anger replaces my despair. I demand, "Tell me now who are you!"

My mom, no, Maranda speaks, "No one can erase our memories. Look at me, Johnny. I am Maranda Boggs, your mother." Memories flash, my heart aches.

The old woman slaps her. "How dare you claim the prince as your own!"

Maranda hides her face and cries. I want to defend my mom, but she's not my mom. She's a liar. I stand there and stare, fighting against the pull of my body to collapse on the floor.

The old woman screams at me, "She's a traitor! When you were a small child, the Guardians kidnapped you and hid you among the humans. We have all been waiting for the return of the prince," she snaps her eyes toward Maranda, "so that we can punish the ones who kidnapped you from your mother, the queen."

Her words pound through my brain. *Your mother, the queen.* I look at my mom, no Maranda, struggling at the end of the demon's hands. She needs me, but she's the reason I don't know who I am or where I belong. She lied to me all of these years, forcing me to be whom she wanted.

Maranda begs, "Johnny, everything I have done was for your own good." I step back and hit the wall. She cries, "Son—"

My body is shaking. I scream, "Don't call me that! You're not my mother. You're a liar!" I can't look at her. I drop my eyes to glare at the floor and clench my fists.

"Johnny, we had to protect you." Maranda sobs.

"From my real mom?" I laugh in complete anger. "Take her away!"

I turn and fly through the wall into the hallway. Each one of my steps shakes the floor beneath me. This can't be real. This is another nightmare. I need to wake up. I stammer like a drunk man into the main foyer.

The halls are empty. Everyone is gone.

Something in my pocket vibrates. I pull it out and see a digital stopwatch flashing on the cell phone. 00:00.

Footsteps approach, I lift my chin. The man in the black suit is walking toward me. My heart races as if it's in the Kentucky Derby. I'm not ready. I step backward, looking for an exit. My back hits the nurse's desk.

An elevator dings. I have thirty seconds to get there. I drop the phone and sprint, sliding inside the doors just as they close. I grab the rail to brace myself. My chest sends shooting pains throughout my body.

Then a deep voice rings out beside me, "Prince, you have a kingdom to choose."

I jerk my head to see the man in black standing next to me. Impressive. I stand tall to face him.

My fake mom's words ring in my head, "Follow what's inside of you." How am I supposed to follow what's inside of me when everything I know is a lie? The woman I love and trust is not my mother. She's my kidnapper. The queen I have been raised to fight against is my mom. If everything is a lie, then I am a lie.

Nothing is inside of me.

I look at myself in the mirror behind the man in the black suit. There are two reflections staring back at me. My heart stops, then pounds. On the left, I am huge. Ripped abs, bulging muscles, standing tall, holding a scythe covered in a black vine leading to a curved, serrated-edged angel blade. I'm a frickin' beast! My black leather boots, gloves, and upper armor are all covered in curved blades sticking out like thorns on a rose stem. A black vine twists around my body and up my spine, forming a crown covered in black diamonds on the top of my head between two huge horns protruding from my temples curling into a sharp point. My free hand is clenched. Water seeps out from between my fingers, forming a puddle that flows toward my other reflection.

My heart literally feels like it could explode as I look over to see an equally stout body sculpted with gold armor covered in Shamayim carvings. Blue flames leap out of my golden crown, engulfing two huge wings that tower over my shoulders. Imagine the speed and power I will have with a body like that! Like a boss, I stand there holding a sword with a forty-inch high carbon blade glowing with magic. With my free hand, I'm holding the wind, spiraling a ball of power in my palm.

How am I supposed to choose when I don't even know who I am? I stare at both of my reflections, wishing I could interrogate them, but all they do is silently glare at me. I move closer to the mirror and look at myself as the Prince of Light. If I stay in the Kingdom of Light, I will know exactly what to do and how to do it. Everyone will know who I am. It will be a fulfilling, but predictable life. I know that's what everyone expects, but now I'm free to do whatever I want. This is my chance.

I raise my eyebrows and turn my gaze to the dark prince. The Kingdom of Darkness will be a new start in a world opposite the light. No one will know who I was, only who I am. I will have power and riches and anything else I want handed to me. No more sacrificing to help others. The spiraling wind around my light side pulls the blue flames into a fireball in my golden hand. The water from my dark side inches closer, hungry to extinguish the flames forever.

Light and dark cannot coexist. Am I willing to lose the people who are so close to me, but betrayed me? My thoughts drift to Maranda. I can't help but love her and at the same time hate her. Why did she lie to me? They all lied to me.

The vines start to move across my dark side, ready to overtake the light. The blue flames arch around my gold armor ready to fight. Soon the choice will be made for me or I will destroy myself.

I take a deep breath.

He asks, "Which one will it be: the Kingdom of Light or the Kingdom of Darkness?"

Choose Your Kingdom

JOHNNY HAS A choice to make and he must make it now.

Will he choose to stay with the Johnsons and be the Prince of Light, or will he give up everything to be the Prince of Darkness? His choice will affect his entire existence, our entire existence. The Kingdom of Light, Shamayim, offers friends who will stick closer than a brother. The Kingdom of Darkness, Dunabi, offers riches and power over the entire world. No matter which kingdom he chooses, there will be sacrifices. Which direction will he go? Who is he willing to lose?

Take this quiz to help Johnny choose a kingdom.

CITIZEN QUIZ

1. If you saw a stranger hurt, would you
    a. stop and help them,
    b. call for someone else to help, or
    c. keep going?

2. If you saw a friend hurt, would you
    a. stop and help them,
    b. call for someone else to help, or
    c. keep going?

3. If you saw someone drop a large amount of money, would you
    a. run to give it back to them,
    b. call out to them hoping they wouldn't hear you, or
    c. take it (you snooze you lose)?

4. If your friend was being blamed for something you did, would you
    a. tell the truth even if you got in trouble,
    b. lie and get you both out of trouble, or
    c. laugh and walk away?

5. You hear a rumor, and you immediately
    a. stop the person spreading it,
    b. listen and only tell your close friends, or
    c. laugh and tell everyone.

6. You are running late, and you tell everyone
    a. the truth,
    b. a little white lie about traffic, or
    c. your grandma died.

7. You are hungry and someone left a new candy bar on the table, would you

    a. take it to them,

    b. leave it there and check in ten minutes, or

    c. eat it?

8. You hear that someone is getting a divorce, you think,

    a. *That is so sad,*

    b. *That will never happen to me,* or

    c. *Good for them?*

9. You want to go to the mall, but your friend wants to go watch a movie, would you

    a. go to a movie,

    b. find a compromise that makes you happy, or

    c. go to the mall with or without them?

10. Your friend is sick in the hospital, would you

    a. immediately go see them,

    b. Facebook them, or

    c. do nothing (Who cares)?

Tally: As _____ Bs _____ Cs _____

MOSTLY AS: KINGDOM OF LIGHT

You honestly care more about others than yourself. You would be a powerful citizen of Shamayim. You are dependable and willing to go the extra mile. You could possibly be one of the twelve! Turn to page 291 to enter the Kingdom of Light!

MOSTLY AS AND BS: KINGDOM OF LIGHT

You care about others, but you are quick to compromise. Your preference is the easy way out, which will inhibit your ability to be a strong warrior for Shamayim. Find your passion and fight for it! By the tips of your wings, you may enter Shamayim, but take heed, you can fall into the dark. Turn to page 291 to enter the Kingdom of Light.

MOSTLY BS AND CS: KINGDOM OF DARKNESS

You care about yourself and looking good. You do not want to create problems, but you are not willing to help someone in need. All of your focus is on yourself and what you need. You definitely belong with the self-promoting citizens of Dunabi. Beware, Troglodytes will eat the weak for dinner. Enter at your own risk. Go to page 311 to enter the Kingdom of Darkness.

Mostly Cs: Kingdom of Darkness

You only care about you! Whatever can make you look good and feel good is your top priority. If others get in your way, then you step over or on them to get to the top. You definitely belong with the Troglodytes! Turn to page 311 to enter the Kingdom of Darkness!

THE KINGDOM OF LIGHT

THE ELEVATOR DOOR opens.

The world before me is like nothing I have ever imagined. The sky is green, the grass is blue, trees are short, and buildings are huge. I step out and feel the warmth from the blue suns. To my right is a city, but it's silent. To my left is an open field with enough tables and chairs to seat thousands.

"Johnny," comes a sweet voice from behind me.

I turn and see Danielle standing there with a huge smile. I open my arms and she falls right in.

"I was so afraid you wouldn't come back," her voice quakes, fighting tears.

"I told you I would come back for you."

She looks up at me and smiles. "Come with me."

She takes my hand and pulls me over a blue hill and down to a yellow lake. Purple and green ducks swim by a pair of floating cows.

I look at Danielle with a twisted expression.

She shrugs. "Nothing is as it seems."

I chuckle and follow her to a small cottage. When she opens the door, the living room is huge! I hear clanging in the kitchen and voices laughing.

Danielle stops me at the door. "You stay right here. Okay?"

I nod and watch her skip off. Everything feels like home, even the crackling fireplace. Silence catches my attention. I look to the back of the room and see a line of people staring at me. Susan, Ray, Caylee, Ms. Sara, Maestro, and even Mrs. Martinez. I step forward and find my legs sprinting for them. They wrap me up in a hug, sniffling and carrying on about losing me.

I grab Caylee. "I'm sorry about Canyon."

She looks at me funny. Then I feel a huge slap on my back. "Why, bro? What did you do to me now?"

I turn and grab Canyon. Tears will not stay back. "I saw you on the floor. How are you alive?"

"No worries, dude. You just killed my human body. It was a dud anyway." Canyon's face is so serious.

Caylee smacks him on the head. "I keep telling you it wasn't the body that held you back."

My eyes widen. Canyon looks at me and shrugs. "What can I say?"

Everyone starts laughing and sniffling.

Ms. Sara walks over to me. "We found your father."

I drop my head. "He's not my father."

She scowls. "Johnny, David and Maranda have loved you as their own since you were a small child and I know you love them. What more does it take to qualify as a parent?"

I look up. "Ms. Sara, they lied to me."

"You should blame the Guardians for that, not the Boggs." Her hand is on her hip.

I look down at my hands. "It wasn't right, whoever's to blame. I was led to believe I was their kid, Johnathan Boggs."

A new light enters, overtaking the room. Everyone bows their heads and backs out of the room. I turn to see a man with my color of hair and icy blue eyes, King Sai, my real father. His head almost reaches the ceiling, making me feel completely, insignificantly so small.

He smiles. "Sit down, Johnny."

I follow his directions and sit on the couch. He sits next to me and gets very still.

"I am—"

"I know who you are," I interrupt.

He chuckles. "Of course you do."

"Where have you been...*Dad?*" I turn my face sideways.

He looks down. "Every choice I make has consequences. It was not easy to let you go, but the consequence of keeping you would have destroyed us all."

"How is it possible for a small child to destroy kingdoms?"

He looks at me. "Johnny, you were moving mountains before you were a year old. Your Guardians were amazed at your power. We all were." A smile flashes vanishing into a flat serious line. "The queen began to bring in wizards and sorcerers to teach you their crafts. You mastered each one within hours. Nara wanted more, but you were so young." He shakes his head. "You did not know what you were doing."

I stare at him wanting to hear more, but he stops. "What did I do?"

He takes a deep breath. "You divided light from dark."

My head spins. An uncontrollable rambling takes over. "If I divided it, then I can put it back together. I can fix this. Just call back the wizards and sorcerers. I will study and find the answer. I will—"

King Sai puts his hand on my shoulder. "Son, you cannot fix what does not want to be repaired.

Queen Nara has become obsessed with the dark. She wants complete power, to reign over us all. She knows the only one with the power to destroy the light is you."

My breaths huff out of my lungs one after another. This cannot be an absolute, everything can be changed.

He takes his hand off of my shoulder. "I had to move you somewhere safe, for your own good and for the safety of our people. David and Maranda were the perfect human couple. They loved you the moment the Guardians handed you to them. No one from Shamayim knew where you were taken, not even me. For the last fifteen years, the Guardians have remained on earth watching over you and the Boggs, sacrificing everything to protect you."

"Why didn't you protect me here at home?"

"Son, your power is above all, even your mother's and mine. We had to remove you from the spirit world until you were old enough to understand the consequences of your choices."

My eyebrows rise as I sit completely still. I do not feel powerful.

I hear footsteps enter the room. I turn to see my fake mother. My heart escalates my blood flow. Anger manifests inside of me. I feel faint.

Maranda rushes to my side. "Johnny, it will be okay. Just slow your breathing." She strokes my face like she has a million times before when I'm sick, hurt, or angry.

Her voice calms me. I look into her eyes and remember the care, the fun, the *love*. How can she still love me? I take in slow deep breaths and close my eyes. Memories flood my mind of all the times my parents picked me up when I fell down, encouraged me not to give up when I couldn't hit the ball, and taught me how to catch my first fish. Ending with an image of my dad still chained to a wall, *for me*. Willing to die *for me*. All this time, it was all about saving *me*.

I open my eyes and let go of all the anger.

I let go.

Mom wraps her arms around me and sobs. Between muffles, she says, "I thought I lost you."

Her chest heaves as she fights back waves of tears. "I love you more than anything, Johnny. I am so sorry that I tried to cover up who you really were. Even though I was trying to protect you, I should have found a way to tell you the truth."

I sit up. "Mom," her eyes light up, "I know who I really am." She grabs me and squeezes all of the air out of my lungs.

"But you had a right to know." She ducks her head.

"I understand now. You had to follow protocol."

Mom looks up at me, a slow smile forming. "Protect the twelve."

I smile back and nod. *Protect the twelve.* My dad has pounded that in my head since I was young. But what about him? Who protects him? I look at my mom. "What about Dad?" I turn and look at the king. "We need to save him."

King Sai walks over to the door and motions for me to follow. "Prince."

My Mom hugs me and mumbles a lot of I love yous. I stand up and look back at her. "Thank you for all that you have done for me even when I didn't believe in you." My head drops.

My mom says, "Johnny, we will always be here for you, no matter what."

I smile and nod. King Sai opens the cabin door. I follow him out and step into a bright light. I feel a rush of wind in my face as we pass through a light portal and I stumble to a stop. We are standing on a cliff overlooking Shamayim. The city streets wrap around the forests and by the river. People look so happy, spending their time in a worry-free world walking among Celestials. A pure calm rests on the city.

King Sai points across the land. "These are your people. Each citizen of Shamayim has toiled on Earth caring for the needs of others above themselves. Now, they enjoy eternal Utopia under our protection."

I ask, "What are we protecting them from?"

He points to the east. "The darkness is rising." I see a dark cloud drawing near Shamayim. He looks at me. "Times are changing. No longer will peace reign without a fight. The time will come when you will bring the lost home."

I look across the horizon, knowing my dad is still out there. The bright colors are fighting against the darkness approaching. My jaw sets. I don't know if he can hear me, but I send a message to him anyway. *Don't give up, Dad. I will come for you and bring you home.*

"Johnathan, you will have to rise above the darkness to protect your people. Fight the good fight, run the distance so that you may obtain the reward."

I take a deep breath and watch a family running across a blue field laughing and playing with their zebra-printed leopard. They are so happy and it's up to me to keep it that way. How am I supposed to do that when nothing has changed? I'm still the same scrawny teenage boy as I have always been.

King Sai put his hand on my shoulder. A cool breeze blows across my face, entering into my body. I feel it spread throughout every tissue and cell. I close my eyes and see bright colors dancing across my eyelids. Pure joy and a strong peace fill my core. I am the one who prevails. I will protect them from all darkness.

I open my eyes. King Sai is standing proud looking at me. No longer am I peering up to see the king. We are eye to eye. I look down at my huge legs covered in Shamayim armor. I lift my arms, the rays of light bounce off of my huge biceps. I am a beast!

King Sai laughs. "This is who you are. Prince Johnathan, son of King Sai."

I'm standing next to the king with my shoulders back and chin high.

He pats me on the back. "Follow me."

We pass through light to the blue open field with tables and chairs, but this time it is crawling with Shamayim warriors, Celestials, and human souls.

"Come, meet your family, your warriors, your kingdom."

As we approach the festivities, I see Caylee and Canyon standing next to the beautiful Danielle. Her eyes light up when she sees the new me. I want to flex and show a little firepower, but everyone else is watching me too. Maybe later.

King Sai leads me to the head table with my mom seated nearby. As we approach, five bolts of lightning strike delivering the other five Descendants. The first is a bright yellow beam of light shining from a pure spirit. The second is a dark violet slender creature with six gold wings encircled by purple doves. Next, a beautiful girl with long white hair and pink skin glides in and sits down next to King Sai. Her wings glow, casting an orb of light all around her. Following her is a gorgeous brunette with a crown of flowers and seven fairies by her side. The final Descendant is a large man with dark hair and wings of a pure white light. He holds a sword, glowing with magic. He sits on the other side of King Sai leaving a seat open for me.

I sit down beside the man, my brother.

He looks at me and sticks out his hand. "I'm Gabe."

I grab his hand. "Johnny."

He chuckles. "I know, we've been waiting for your return for thousands of years."

My eyes pop out. "Seriously?"

"Yes, brother. You were a small child when the Guardians moved you into hiding. Sixteen human years may not seem like a long time, but consider that every time you blink on Earth, an hour has passed here in Shamayim. Now that's a long time."

"I can't believe that much time has passed. I've missed so much." I drop my head.

Gabe puts his hand on my back. "Trust me, you have not missed anything that you needed to see.

Eternity is a long time. I'm just glad to have you back."

I look up at him and recognize the blue eyes. They're just like mine.

King Sai stands. Silence spills over the crowd. "Citizens of Shamayim, we have waited for this day for many centuries. Our young Prince Johnathan has returned!" Celestials, spirits, human souls, and the Guardians rise to their feet and cheer.

I shift in my seat and stare at King Sai. A yellow flash catches my eye, smiling at me from across the table.

King Sai continues, "In celebration of my son's return, we feast!"

Every table is instantly covered in fruits, vegetables, pastas, and loaves of bread. The next two hours pass quickly filled with childhood stories of magic. My eyes cannot stay away from Danielle. She swings her hair over her shoulder and throws her head back, laughing at Canyon. Beautiful.

A group of human souls pull out guitars, fiddles, banjos, and other instruments. They play upbeat bluegrass music that gets everyone on their feet and dancing in the field. Danielle locks eyes with me.

Gabe slugs my arm. "Go on, brother!"

I teleport from my seat, standing with a big smile right in front of her.

Danielle jumps back, but leans forward the moment she realizes it's me. "Well, hello there, handsome." She smiles.

I take her hand and spin her around. She laughs. We take center stage on the field and two-step our hearts out. I love to watch her eyes as she laughs and gazes back at me. The music slows down. I pull her close. She smells so sweet.

"Johnny?"

"Danielle."

She chuckles and rolls her eyes up at me. "Are you happy?"

My brow crumples. "Of course! Aren't you?"

"Yes, as long as I am with you."

"Well, that's good news because I don't plan on letting you go."

She smiles and snuggles her face into my chest. I hear a sniffle. "Please don't ever leave me."

I stop dancing and lift her chin. A tear rolls down her cheek. "Danielle, I will never leave you."

"I know you wouldn't on purpose, but what if someone hurts you or kills you?"

"What would make you think that?"

She drops her head. "I know they're coming."

"Who?"

"The dark."

My stomach rolls. "How do you know that?"

"When I was in Dunabi, I heard them. They're going to attack with or without your help."

I kiss her on the forehead. "There's no need to worry about tomorrow when we have today."

She pulls me close to her. I want to promise to protect her and always be together, but I also know they're coming.

The music picks back up. We dance a few more songs, but I can see that Danielle has lost her real smile. I walk with her back to her table, but she pulls me another direction. There's a beautiful lake, so clear that you can see the fish swim by, dogfish that really look like dogs, catfish, seahorses, and other creatures that I've never seen before. We sit by the water's edge and I wrap my arm around her.

"Do you ever wonder why we're here?"

I move her hair out of her eyes. "All the time."

"There has got to be a reason all of this is happening."

"Only the king knows and I doubt he will be disclosing the greater plan anytime soon."

"Why not?"

"Everything we do is a journey, our journey. We make choices and deal with the consequences. It's up to us to choose our own path."

"But how do we know where we're going when it's all such a big secret?"

I laugh. "I guess that's part of the surprise."

We watch the water dance around. The trees sway in the wind and blue leaves fall.

"Watch this." I put my hands together and swirl them around. As soon as I open them, a wind funnel forms in my palms. Danielle's eyes light up.

"Can I touch it?"

I laugh. "Sure."

She inches one finger closer and closer until she reaches the edge of the wind. It whips her finger like touching the blades of a ceiling fan. She jerks her hand back with a loud laugh. I increase the size of the funnel and sit it on the grass next to her. She watches it dance with wide eyes. I make it jump over a few rocks and throw some water onto us. Then I let it fade into nothing.

"That's so cool! What else can you do?"

"Am I a magic pony trick, now?"

She nods her head and sits up on her knees expecting more. I see a strong tree behind her. It will be perfect. I twist my wrist. Blue flames dance from my fingertips. Danielle covers her mouth with her hands and watches closely as I throw it over her shoulder. She gasps and twists around to see the tree engulfed in blue fire.

"Johnny! You're gonna burn the tree down."

"No, I'm not. Look closer."

She stands up and walks toward the tree. "Can I touch it?"

"At your own risk."

She cocks her head sideways. I smile and nod. Her finger gets within a foot of the flames and one jumps out and touches her. She jumps back and hides behind me.

"What are you hiding from? It's not going to hurt you. Well, not as long as I don't tell it to."

"What is it?"

"It's me."

She steps around and looks in my eyes. "How?"

"The power of emotion."

She walks away from me and approaches the tree. She puts her hand into the flames and stands there with her eyes closed. Her other hand lifts and enters the flames. Then her entire body disappears. I drop my fire and run to her. She's standing there completely still.

"Danielle, are you okay?" I grab her shoulders.

A slow smile spreads across her face. "You do love me."

She opens her eyes and slaps her arms around me. All in one movement, she presses her lips onto mine. I slip my fingers into her hair and gently kiss her. She pulls my body closer. I do love her. The ground beneath us shakes. I can feel her chest heaving. She twists one of her legs around mine. I pick her up and move under the cover of the tree.

The tree is vibrating and rocks are splashing into the water. I crumple my brow and open my eyes. The light around us is flashing in and out like a light bulb burning out.

Canyon and Caylee appear beside me. Caylee orders, "The king needs you."

I tell the twins as I point to Danielle, "Stay with her."

They nod. Danielle grabs my arm. "Don't leave me."

I pull her in. "I will always come back for you. I promise."

I hear her sniffling as I teleport to the king's table. All of the Descendants are seated around a wooden table. In the center is a large glass orb. Inside is a large amount of movement. I look closer. It's the earth.

The king speaks, "They did not give us much time. The south has been split wide open and the Troglodytes have started infiltrating the humans in massive numbers." He waves his hand over the orb showing the huge earthquake that split the ground wide open. Like insects swarming, Troglodytes of all sizes are crawling out and spreading across the land. Then he zooms in on Godley High School. The Troglodytes are attacking. "We must make a decision. There has always been a battle for human souls, but now they are going after them in full force. We either hope the human soul can withstand the darkness or we go in and fight."

Gabe steps up. "Humans are easily tempted. They will not see the Troglodytes for who they are."

My sister, Charlie, is glowing with fury. Her pink skin and white hair are pulsating a bright light. "We cannot sit back and hope for the best. The humans need us. We are their protectors."

Zada speaks as if she is singing a hypnotizing tune, "We are made for peace, not war."

The yellow light across the table ignites into flames. Jophiel's voice shakes the room. "We do not ask for war, but we do not back down when called to fight. We are a peaceful kingdom, but we are not weak."

I watch the Troglodytes crawling up the stairs and entering my school. My friends are inside there. I cannot sit back and watch this happen. "Let me go back."

King Sai smiles.

Gabe charges, "What good will that do?"

"I can show them the way. They are my friends, my family."

Jophiel questions, "How can one person save the world?"

"I have to try. If we go in there fighting, light against dark, many humans will lose their minds.

Their souls will be permanently damaged. I can go and show them the way and the truth."

Charlie looks at me. "Johnny, you will be putting yourself in the middle of a war. They will attack you and kill you."

"Then so be it. I have to go back."

൭ഝ൭

To be continued.

THE KINGDOM OF DARKNESS

THE ELEVATOR DOORS open.

I don't feel or look any different. Maybe it takes a few minutes to morph into beast mode. I step out onto a balcony and look at my arms. Still scrawny. There's an active casino below with hundreds of creatures playing their hand at games of chance. Some are seated at table games, drinking and laughing and drinking some more. Others are stumbling up to slot machines placing their bets on a coin and screaming whether they win or lose. Off of the main floor, I see private rooms branching off for poker, shows, and more slot machines.

Everyone is consumed within their world, they don't notice the arrival of their prince. I step forward and look over the railing. Anger is swelling inside of me. This is not the greeting I was expecting. A flash of blond hair moves through two trolls. I watch the elegant creature move through the people, hoping she will turn to face me. The music pounds in my chest bringing back strong desire. My patience is gone. I head toward the stairs to find the girl.

A door opens behind me. I look over my shoulder. Unable to breathe, I smile. Shay glides toward me. I take her into my arms. Neither of us speaks as her lips meet mine. The bells, screaming, music, and all other sounds from the casino disappear. I am completely consumed by her.

Time holds us together until broken apart by a loud voice, "Back up, you two! There's enough time for that later."

I pull away from Shay and open my eyes to see Caylee, smirking at me with her hand on her hip. She looks like an Amazon warrior with huge muscles. Metal and leather protect the necessary organs while leaving the perfect amount of skin exposed to distract her opponent. She's built better than I am! I'm so ready to be the man I saw in the elevator mirror. No such luck, I'm stuck as a human teenager. Ugh!

I reach around Shay and grab Caylee in a big hug and whisper in her ear, "I will always miss Canyon."

She pushes back. "Why?"

"You won't?" My head tilts to the side and I look her square in the eyes. A bright sparkle forms in her eyes.

Suddenly, something slugs me on the back. A deep voice asks, "You planning to take me out again?"

I feel like a young boy turning around to wrestle my younger brother. With a big smile, I twist around and grab Canyon in a headlock, messing up his long hair. He slips out of my grip and pulls my leg out from under me. I'm surprised at the size of his muscles and how tall he is.

I jump to catch myself and hold onto his shoulders. "I'm not going down that easy."

Canyon laughs. "Good, cause neither am I!" He puts my leg down and leans on the rail.

"How's it possible?" I ask.

Canyon rolls his eyes. "It was no big deal. You just let my human form die."

I'm not sure whether to laugh or apologize.

"Come on, big guy, you have a kingdom to meet." Canyon walks down the stairs.

Shay and Caylee follow him, leaving me standing there. I look over the rail. Everyone is moving toward the base of the stairs. I've never seen such a crowd. Some are small and hunched over, darting around the room. Others are gigantic, pushing through like army tanks. Their faces have battle scars and burns. Some do not appear to have any human features left at all, if they were ever human.

I walk down the stairs and a deep voice roars, "Hail, Prince Johnathan, the one who prevails!"

The crowd erupts. I pause on the last step as they crowd around me. Canyon and Caylee are on each side of me. Shay takes my arm and walks with me into the crowd. Creatures are grunting and reaching for me. My face is hard as I look at each of them in passing. They're damaged, but strong, fighters that will not give up and will remain loyal to the death.

Then I see a beautiful face and then another mixed in the crowd of beasts. Their skin is perfect and smooth. Their eyes are magical. Long, red hair flows down their backs moving across their rock-hard bodies. Each one has three horns, two swirling out of the sides of their head like mine and then one straight horn on the front. Demons!

Standing in the back, I see creatures with two huge horns twisting up from their scalp. They are covered in scales and have large eyes and wide mouths full of teeth. Multiple tentacles sway behind their massive dragon wings coming off of their human arms. A guttural growl vibrates from their core.

Another growl catches my eye. The beast is huge, covered in a coarse fur that looks sharp enough to cut through anything that touches it. Small horns jut out of its brow outlining its hungry eyes. Its mouth protrudes with the teeth of a lion. Next to it is a sultry beast. Its flesh clings to its bones. I do not see its mouth, just bones layered over bones on its jaw. Eyes peer through a hollow space with huge ram horns taking over its forehead and rolling down the back of its neck.

Shay leads me into a grand ballroom with long banquet tables covered in every delicacy imaginable. The creatures move from table to table taking whatever they want. The music stops. Everyone, including Shay and the twins, bows. I turn to look across the room and see Queen Nara, my mother, gliding into the room with guards on each side of her. Close behind are the six Descendants. They approach the head table and are seated. No one in the room moves.

The queen holds her hand out. I hear her speak inside of my mind, *Come, my son. I have waited long enough to have you by my side once again.* She smiles.

Warmth consumes my body. I move away from Shay. The Descendants stare at me with dark faces. Angry. The moment I reach the queen, she wraps her arms around me. I can feel her energy surging into my body, giving me power and authority. My body burns, every muscle twitches. I open my eyes and look down. The beast has arrived.

No longer are my arms and legs twigs. I am huge. I hold my hands up and clench my fists, watching my muscles flex with each movement. I am covered in black leather and blades. Perfect.

I look at the queen, smiling as she turns to the bowing crowd. "Rise and worship your prince!"

The room rustles with movement as they lift their eyes to see me standing before them and then the entire room gasps. The huge beasts are now my size, looking at me eye to eye. I find Shay, she looks at me in terror and shock. I smile, trying to comfort her. The longer she looks at me, the faster a smile spreads across her face.

She screams, "Behold Prince Johnathan!"

Cheers and chants spread across the ballroom and throughout the casino. Every creature is cheering, except for the Descendants. They are sitting, lifeless, staring at the crowd with jaws clenched.

The queen motions for me to sit down beside her. The empty table in front of me is suddenly covered in a feast fit for Vikings. I grab a turkey leg, but before I can take a bite, the queen rises and claps twice in the air. A flash of magic pulsates through the room, changing everyone into human form, except Canyon. He turns into a ghost and drops his pork chop to the dirt floor. He looks straight at me and I hear his voice in my head, *No prob, bro, you go ahead and eat. Don't worry about me starving!* He cocks his head and glares. I nod and dive into the feast before me.

I look around the room. Everyone is gorgeous, like supermodel gorgeous. The hunchbacks all the way to the huge creatures have transformed into magazine-quality humans.

The queen says, "Much better." She leans over. "There's nothing worse than listening to beasts consume a meal." She chuckles.

We spend hours eating and then the real party gets started. The lights drop and the music pumps throughout the room. It's complete chaos like a rave gone wild. I love it!

I dance with Shay despite the multiple advances from creatures, small and large. The air is intoxicating everyone, causing a hallucinogenic atmosphere. Everyone is laughing and partying with no curfew in sight.

Someone growls in my head, *Prince, your presence is requested.*

I turn and see one of the Descendants standing by a door looking directly at me. The queen passes through the door with the other Descendants following. I look down at Shay and tell her, "Business calls." I lift her chin and kiss her, but she does not let me go. I get lost in the moment and assume the meeting can wait five more minutes. Our bodies wrap together. I forget that anyone else is in the room. Her body moves against mine. Now this is heaven.

A voice jars my mind, *A request was made. Do not tempt me, Prince!*

My eyes widen. The voice tries to intimidate me, but he only ignites my rage. I let go of Shay and dart across the room and through the door. I'm standing in a meeting room with a map of earth on the huge wooden table. Each Descendant is in their spiritual form. I see one of each beast sitting around the table. There is only one open seat, for me. I sit next to the queen, feeling every eye glaring at me.

The queen announces, "The era of darkness has arrived." She smiles at me. "We will prevail."

The room is completely silent.

She looks down at the map. "We have infiltrated the west. Shamayim warriors have a stronghold over the north and east. Our next target, the south." She points to Texas. "Shamayim is weak. The time is now."

The hunchback grumbles, "We should be discreet. Take them in the night when the light is away."

The leviathan gargles a laugh. "Wait for the light! They should fear us. I will wait for no one."

The queen mediates, "We are not waiting for anything. Our strategy is flawless, if everyone commits to the plan." She darts her eyes to the beast with tentacles and wings.

He looks at her and smiles. I can hear him seething through his layers of teeth, "My queen, I will do only what I think is best for our kingdom."

A young girl with a thin layer of skin covering her bones curls up in her chair and smiles. "Beal, that is what we are afraid of, *you thinking*."

I want to laugh, but Beal does not allow it. He screams, "There is no option, but war! Why are we pussy footing around them? Let's take our world and theirs!"

The wolf slams his fist on the table. "We move in the dark. I will not submit to the light. They have our people confined to the abyss claiming war crimes. Well, I think it is time to take them back!"

The beautiful demon speaks in a soothing voice, calming the wolf. "Amon, we will set our people free, in due time."

The leviathan looks at me with a sharp glare and mocks, "What do you think, oh prevailing one?"

My huge muscles flex. I feel complete anger pulse through me. A deep rumble comes from within me. I glare at the beast, "We attack, now." The moment the words leave my mouth, the ground shakes.

The queen rises, "Then we attack."

The other Descendants rise one by one. As each stands, the ground trembles violently. The queen waves her hands in the air and down to the floor, creating a wave of wind that encircles the room. The air lifts me and in a flash I am standing on the side of the mountain before millions of beasts. The twins and Shay are near me with solemn faces, ready to do this. The queen and the other Descendants are standing next to me in a perfect line facing the crowd. In front of each Descendant, the creatures of their kind gather, staring at their leader. Beal raises his weapon, chanting and grunting for war. Like dominoes, we all raise our swords and scythes. The darkness shakes with our impending reign of terror.

Adrenaline races through my veins and arteries, pumping every muscle to life. I am ready to fight, to right all of the wrongs done to me. Anger no longer manifests inside of me, it *is* me.

The queen raises her staff, and silence falls across the Troglodytes of all races.

She declares, "Warriors of Dunabi, the time has come. Our prince and your royals of darkness declare that Shamayim has committed the highest of war crimes, taking innocent prisoners of war. It is time that we bring our brothers and sisters home."

The chanting of the beasts escalate to screams. I see something scurrying among their heels. The tiny Troglodytes with red eyes are everywhere, jumping and waving their weapons.

She screams, "This very hour, we attack!" Every creature pounds their feet against the mountain.

The queen slams her staff into the ground. The vines twisting around her begin to move. I feel movement from my body and look down to see my vines crawling across the ground. Each Descendant extends their vines to join the queen's. They unite and wrap up into one large black root that digs into the mountain, breaks away the stones, and opens the face of a cave. The other Descendants, the queen, and I walk into the cave and form a circle. Our vines crawl up the cave wall and cover its ceiling.

She lifts her staff to the center. Each Descendant follows her lead and lifts their weapons. I am the last to raise my scythe, casting electricity through our circle that pulsates through each vine. Power flows in and out of my body, uniting with my brothers and sisters. Suddenly, our united force blows a hole above our heads, allowing a dim light to shine through.

The electricity calms. We lower our arms. Each Descendant is breathing deeply, but I'm ready to rock and roll. I look at the queen. She smiles. "Johnathan, you will lead the way." I feel the glares of my brothers and sisters burning with envy through my back. I do not care.

I jump up and out of the cave into a graveyard. Caylee, Canyon, and Shay are right behind me. We stand back and watch the tiny troglodytes scurry out of the opening like a million spiderlings hatching. One by one, each Descendant along with their creatures rises from the ground. Beasts are crushing the gravestones underfoot and ripping caskets out of the ground while growling for their orders. Once we are all assembled, I lift my scythe. "Citizens of Darkness, we will hit the Light where it hurts the most, human souls. Go and find empty souls to take!"

The dark army is unleashed.

To be continued.